CHASING HOME: CHRISTIAN CONTEMPORARY ROMANCE

TRIPLE STAR RANCH ROMANCE, BOOK 1

EMMA WOODS

CONTENTS

I USED the gas station bathroom that was only mildly disgusting compared to some, and then walked around the store, stretching my legs. In all my traveling, I'd developed a fondness for gas stations that baffled many people. There's just something about a little oasis in the midst of the endless highway system that makes me feel a camaraderie with other travelers.

Sure, they might be dirty and a bit stinky. I have most certainly used their bathrooms to hone my hovering skills. Still, I adore the glistening hot dogs shining under their heat lamps, the orangey nacho cheese with its dry top layer, and the liquid-magma-hot toffee cappuccino that pours out of the machine and always threatens to scald your hand if you move your cup the wrong way.

This was my last planned stop before arriving in Birch Springs, Wyoming. I had to make the most of it.

So, I grabbed a large bag of chips and a soda in a Styrofoam cup the size of Rhode Island, and I couldn't resist buying a stiff, nylon baseball cap in shades of neon that boasted "Esto Perpetua" with the outline of the state of Idaho. I happened to know that "esto perpetua" was the state motto of Idaho, and that it meant "Let it be perpetual." Since I didn't know when I'd be in this state again, I simply had to add the cap to my cheesy-gas-station-state-memento collection.

Soon I was back in my Dodge Caravan, rolling down the road toward my new adventure, the wind caressing my face through the open windows. Since my long, almost-black hair was tucked up under my new ball cap, I didn't have to worry about it blowing into my face.

I couldn't stop myself from grinning. Man, this was what I loved.

There are some things you should know about me. My name is Emily McBride. I'm twenty-six years old. I love running, traveling, and meeting new people. I'm five-foot-seven and slim, which is probably in part due to my Chinese grandmother. She also contributed to my dark, stick-straight hair and brown almond-shaped eyes. My three Irish grandparents contributed the pale skin and freckles.

But, what's most important to know is that I committed some years back to never owning more than I could easily carry in my car, and to never live anywhere for more than a year. I have three pairs of shoes. Seriously. My one splurge is my state memento collection. I happen to own a magnet from Vermont, a glass dragon with "Nebraska" on it (why would someone put "Nebraska" on a glass dragon?), and a really ugly stuffed pig wearing a Louisiana t-shirt, in addition to a number of articles of clothing with various state mottos splashed across their fronts. I also own a pair of socks with palmetto trees on them from South Carolina.

I know what you're thinking: why would anyone choose to live this way? To be honest, I don't really tell a lot of people about my commitment to the nomadic life, because most people look at me like I must be crazy when I tell them. So I mostly keep that quiet and just move on when I'm ready.

I think growing up as an army brat was a major contributor. I was born in Hawaii, and my family proceeded to live in Kansas, Germany, Texas, North Carolina, and South Carolina as we followed my dad around the world throughout his career. When I went off to college in Michigan, I found myself chafing that I had to live in the same place for four years. I spent every vacation traveling, volunteering, and basically escaping the same old scenery I saw every day.

The minute I had my diploma in hand, I packed my minivan and drove off into the sunset. Okay, not actually the sunset, but you get my drift. Since leaving school five years ago, I've spent significant periods of time in Iowa, Illinois, Texas, California, and most recently, Oregon.

As I drove along the almost-empty Idaho highway, I reflected on my time in Oregon. I'd worked for the parks department, putting my love of the outdoors and my biology degree to good use. It hadn't paid enough to make rent, so I'd also worked part-time at one of Oregon's plethora of coffee shops. I was proud to now boast superior barista skills.

While I found the work interesting and made some very nice acquaintances who bordered on friends, after nine months, I was itching to move on. I always know it's time to go when I start scouring job boards online, looking for opportunities in distant places.

I had been thrilled to stumble across an ad for a barista job at the Birch Springs Beanery in Birch Springs, Wyoming. The shop was owned by a Mr. Matthew Donovan, who also roasted his own beans. It sounded like the sort of place for which I was well groomed. I'd spent too much time around coffee snobs to be able to work anywhere less millennial.

After a video conference interview, I put in my notice at my other jobs. It turned out that Matt was about my age and was able to recommend a house that rented rooms in town. I was used to dingy apartments and dated rental houses. Renting a room sounded like a great adventure. When Matt mentioned that his younger sister lived there and loved it, I decided to contact the owner. Now, just two weeks later, I was headed toward the next stop on my life's journey. In fact, I was feeling rather poetic about the whole thing.

I saw signs for the exit just as I slurped the last of my soda. I flipped on my blinker and puttered onto the exit ramp. A quick glance down at my trusty road atlas told me to turn left to get to Birch Springs.

I suppose I should mention that I don't like technology much. I have a dinky flip phone that I keep in my glove box for emergencies. And texting. It makes it much easier to stay independent when I don't have the ability to be reached by people who want to "grab coffee" or "get together sometime." I have a laptop for using the internet, and my brain and an atlas for GPS. I suppose it's unusual, but it suits me.

Driving the 6.2 miles from the highway to Birch Springs was very enjoyable. I flipped my old iPod to my Dolly Parton playlist and watched the wide open land ripple past on all sides of me. There were mountains off in the distance whose white tops seemed to greet me with a friendly salute.

I'd seen cattle farms in Iowa and sheep ranches in Oregon. I wasn't sure what type of ranches I was passing now, since I saw miles of fence but no actual animals. Still, it was picturesque country and I sighed happily. Wyoming would suit me well for the next few months.

Birch Springs itself was a cute little town. About a mile and a half from Main Street, the houses began to resemble neighborhoods. I slowed to the required twenty miles per hour and drank in the sight of the small town. There was a Yard of the Month sign proudly displayed on a perfectly manicured lawn. Kids chased each other at the town park. I heard familiar splashes and shouts as I drove past the town pool.

Even though I didn't have to, I took the time to drive down Main Street so that I could see where Birch Springs Beanery was located. I'd told Matt I would meet him there tomorrow, if all went according to plan. To my delight, I saw that the old buildings of the downtown had undergone a renovation and were now adorable little shops. I spotted a drug store, a diner, the old bank, the library, a hardware store, and the Beanery.

On a whim, I pulled into one of the slanted parking spaces in front of the coffee shop and went inside. It was a long, thin building with a spacious café at the front, complete with a raised platform that was probably used for a stage sometimes. I took in the little tables with their pairs of chairs, the long wooden counter with a display of prepackaged snacks, and the hand-lettered menu hung on the far wall. I breathed in the scents of coffee beans, caramel, vanilla, and coconut. The building was old, and the floors creaked as I walked. However, a fresh coat of blue paint and some crisp black-and-white photos set in modern black frames kept the place from feeling out-of-date.

I meandered to the counter, where a high school

girl stood chewing gum and fiddling with a fresh packet of napkins.

"Hi, I'll be with you in a sec," she said, then continued to try and open the napkins.

"Actually, I was wondering if Matt was in. I'm supposed to start work tomorrow."

The girl turned her attention to me, and her mouth dropped open, giving me a full view of her gum. "Oh, wow. Matt literally just told me that you were going to start tomorrow, and here you are. Let me go get him. He's in the office."

She turned and flounced off, sleek ponytail swinging. I grinned ruefully. Had I been like that back in high school? Probably. I rubbed my forehead and chuckled.

Just then, the front door opened and the sound of bells jingled. I glanced back over my shoulder and saw a young man enter, wearing well-cut jeans and a t-shirt that sported a vintage band I was pretty sure he didn't actually listen to. Our eyes met across the café, and I felt a jolt of electricity. He had clear, sea-green eyes that were set in a too-handsome, tanned face.

I stared at him, and my brain stopping working momentarily. However, my appearance clearly did not have this effect on him, since his mouth split into a smile that revealed perfect white teeth.

This was one seriously good-looking guy.

And while I was obviously not immune to his attractiveness, I did have enough experience with such pretty-boy charmers to be able to resist any attempt he might make toward me. Once my brain kicked back into action, that is.

So, when he strode over to the counter and gave me a flirty half-smile, I merely raised an eyebrow.

His smile froze for a second, but my lack of enthusiasm didn't stop him for long. "You're new in town. I'm Nate Weisert. Welcome to Birch Springs. Are you just passing through or here to stay?"

"Emily McBride," I responded coolly. I shook his proffered hand only to be polite. "I'm going to be working here at the Beanery."

He leaned back and slid his hands into his jeans pockets. "Cool. I grew up here, so if you need a tour guide, let me know. Not that there's all that much to see. Small town, you know."

"I noticed," I said shortly.

I settled nonchalantly with my back against the counter, elbows propped on top. Nate took the same stance next to me, our elbows touching. For a moment, his beautiful eyes flashed at me, and I gulped.

But I'd known guys like this before. Nate belonged to that fraternity of men who always had women doing whatever they wanted. They were handsome and flirtatious, and we couldn't seem to resist them. One of my college boyfriends had been very similar to Nate, and things had not ended well. I still remembered the punched-in-the-gut feeling I had when I'd spotted him kissing another girl in the front booth of a restaurant window as I walked past.

Holding that bitterness close, I kept my voice even and said, "Listen, Nate, I appreciate the offer, but I'm not interested."

His eyebrows shot up toward his dark-brown hairline. I got the impression that he wasn't refused very often. He considered me for a few heartbeats, and then offered, "Well, let me know if you change your mind. I come in here for coffee pretty often, so I'm sure we'll see a lot of each other."

"Oh, goody." My sarcasm got the best of me, and I cringed inwardly when his smile fell. I didn't mean to be rude, really. My mouth just got away from me sometimes.

Luckily, the high school girl returned. "Emily, Matt asked you to head back to the office. He's on the phone, but he won't be much longer." She gave me directions, and I scooted around the corner without giving Nate another look.

As I walked toward the hallway heading to the back rooms, I heard Nate say, "Hey, there, Sophie. How's my favorite girl?"

From Sophie's giggle, I knew she'd fallen into his Mr. Charming trap. I rolled my eyes and made a concentrated effort to shove any thoughts of Nate Weisert out of my mind.

The front half of the Beanery was made up of the café, and the back half consisted of storage rooms and offices. I smelled the heavenly scent of coffee beans roasting. Instantly, the tension from my awkward run-in with Nate left my shoulders.

I spotted a large man who had to be Matt Donovan talking on a phone and pacing around a small office. He saw me and waved me in, flashing a welcoming smile. I stepped into the office and looked around as I waited, taking in the messy desk, the untidy bookshelf, and the really cool band poster on the wall. I walked closer and nodded my satisfaction. Unlike Nate, this was undoubtedly a band that Matt actually listened to. It was one I liked too, which cemented my good approval of my boss for life.

"Sorry about that," he said as he returned his phone to his pocket.

I turned and shook hands with Matt. Though we'd had a video conference, there was a lot about him I hadn't realized. Like his completely tattooed arms. He sported two full sleeves of tattoos and even had a few peeking up through the vee of his t-shirt. Matt was a big guy. He towered over me and was clearly a longtime fan of weightlifting. However, his bushy beard and twinkling eyes made him seem more like a giant teddy bear than any sort of threat.

"No problem," I replied. "I noticed you've got a signed poster of Project 86. Nice."

His eyebrows rose. "You like Project?"

"I do. When did you get it signed?"

We talked music for the next ten minutes. My first

impression was confirmed: I liked Matt a lot. He had that big-brother vibe, which I preferred so much to Nate's charmer routine. I had a good feeling about being able to work for him. Who knows? Maybe I'd stay in Birch Springs for a full year this time.

"Are you sure you don't mind opening tomorrow?" he asked once we'd moved on from discussing our favorite bands.

I shrugged. "No problem. If you don't mind showing me the ropes today, I could definitely open tomorrow."

Matt gave me a wide smile, showing off his slightly crooked front teeth. "I knew I hit the lottery when I hired you, Emily!"

"What can I say? I'm a catch," I joked.

My new boss chuckled and motioned for me to follow him. Back up front, Sophie was again popping her gum and restocking the napkin dispenser. Nate Weisert was nowhere in sight, I tried not to notice.

Between Matt and Sophie, I was given a quick introduction to operations at the Beanery. It was pretty standard. Though the cash register was different and the menu was, of course, unique, I got the hang of things without much explanation. Coffee was coffee, and it was made the same way all across America.

Before leaving, Matt gave me a stack of Birch Springs Beanery t-shirts and a set of keys to use for opening in case I beat him there the next morning. He promised to do his best not to leave me hanging, but he seemed extremely relieved that I could handle things if I was on my own.

I bid my new co-workers goodbye and returned to my car. I had every reason to hope that I would have a good work experience here. If only I could stop thinking about Nate's electric eyes, I could call my first stop in my new town a raging success.

2

My grandparents had lived in a small town when I was young, and I'd always liked visiting them. Something about Birch Springs made me feel right at home. As the opening notes of Dolly's "Two Doors Down" came on over the speakers, I eased up on the accelerator and let myself cruise down the streets toward my new home, contentment and excitement filling my heart.

When Matt had told me that his sister lived at the Bumblebee House, I'd wondered what to expect. Having seen Birch Springs for myself, I was beginning to understand how a rooming house for women made sense. There was something sort of old-fashioned about the idea, but Birch Springs was an old-fashioned sort of place.

The road leading up to Bumblebee House was edged by a rough wooden fence, which served as a jungle gym for climbing roses. There was a cheerful iron sign at the entrance to the driveway with a wrought iron bee in a circle. Trees blocked the actual house from view, and I was surprised by the length of the winding driveway once I'd turned off the street. I passed a small, neat cottage and many trees that boasted skirts of tidy flower beds as I drove further from civilization and into what seemed to be a bit of a fairy tale.

Finally, Bumblebee House itself appeared around a curve. My eyebrows rose as I looked over the large Victorian dwelling. There was no question that it was a lovely home. The white paint was immaculate, and the green trim was fresh. The windows gleamed and the front porch seemed to beckon visitors to come inside. There was a round turret on the left side of the house and dormer windows perched jauntily on the roof. Bright flowers filled window boxes, rocking chairs dotted the porch, and even a cozy swing swayed gently in the breeze.

I parked the van and sat looking over the house, dumbstruck. Never in my life had I lived in anything like this. I had to admit that I was a bit intimidated. Dank apartments with stained sinks and not enough windows, I knew how to handle. Here, I half expected a footman to bustle out and open my door for me.

"Here we go," I finally said into the silent car. I threw the strap of my canvas messenger bag over my shoulder, pulled the keys from the ignition, and stepped out onto the red brick pavers, which were laid in a herringbone pattern. After the drive up and the first view of the house, I could only whisper to myself, "Of course the sidewalk of Bumblebee House would be adorable."

I rang the bell and smiled wryly when a pleasant two-note tone announced my arrival inside the house. It wasn't long before footsteps sounded.

The door swung open, and a petite redhead looked up at me, a smile growing across her face. "Hello! You must be Emily." She stuck out a hand. "I'm Mae. I live here, too. You are going to love it. There is no place in the world like Bumblebee House."

I returned her smile and gestured vaguely over my shoulder. "I left my things in the car. I wasn't sure what to do with them."

Mae stepped back and beckoned me in. "Don't worry about that. Come in. Rosa has made tea."

Without further explanation, Mae turned and padded off toward the kitchen. I followed her, my eyes roving as I tried to take it all in. The foyer was full of warm, gleaming wood floors, and an elegant staircase led to the second floor. I glimpsed a formal dining room, a shelf-lined study, and a less formal breakfast area before we turned into the kitchen. Everywhere I looked I saw fascinating artwork, inviting furniture, and a variety of wallpaper that all worked together to create a unique and very welcoming atmosphere.

The question of who Rosa might be was answered

when we reached the kitchen. Behind the hanging copper pots, which hovered over the large kitchen island, stood a woman who must have been in her late 30s or early 40s. She was of medium height and was curvy all over. She had long, dark hair ending in straight-cut bangs above her dark, dramatic brows. Rosa's rich brown eyes twinkled at me, and her dark-red, lipsticked mouth curved into a smile as Mae introduced us.

"I'm so glad to meet you in person," Rosa said in a surprisingly husky voice. "I hope your time here at Bumblebee House is delightful. Would you care for a cup of tea?"

"I would, if I could use the bathroom first." And without further ado, Mae led me through the laundry room and up a few stairs to the little half-bath.

As I washed my hands, I took in a grouping of framed pictures which hung above the towel bar. The pictures were a quirky mix of old and new and worked perfectly with the blue-striped wallpaper. I washed my hands with the rose-scented soap and shook my head in disbelief. This place was something else.

Once I returned to the breakfast room off the kitchen, where Mae and Rosa sat at the table doctoring their individual teacups, I began to understand how this house was such a showplace. There was just something about Rosa that gave off beauty and welcoming at the same time.

"This house belonged to one of the early founders

of Birch Springs," she explained, pushing the little china creamer pitcher toward me. "It was in a near state of ruin when my grandfather bought it thirty years ago. He worked to restore it and asked me to help decorate it, since I was the only grandchild who lived in town. And, well, I have a flair for that sort of thing." She looked as though she was embarrassed to be caught bragging.

I looked over her dramatic makeup and hairstyle, her vintage 50s-inspired floral print dress, and cameo necklace. "I can see that," I nodded.

Mae grinned and waggled her eyebrows at me. "Rosa decorated this entire place. Every year at Christmas, it's part of the Tour of Homes. Everyone for miles around comes to see what she's done."

Rosa waved that off. "When my grandfather died, he left the house to me. It was too much to live in all by myself, so I decided to rent the spare rooms to single women."

Just then, the front door opened, and the sound of women's voices drifted through to us.

"Sounds like the others are home," Rosa said with a smile.

I gulped my tea and braced myself to meet the women who would turn out to be the rest of my new housemates.

I CARRIED the last of my boxes up to my bedroom and laid it next to all the rest of my possessions. With the help of Mae, Rosemarie, and Jill, we'd finished the job in three trips up and down the stairs. This was a particularly good thing, I thought, because I'd chosen the attic bedroom across from Mae. After three treks up to the third floor, we were all glad it was over.

"I can't believe this is everything you own," Jill announced, hands on her hips as she surveyed the six boxes, two suitcases, three bins, and one large duffle bag. "I think I moved in with a dozen suitcases alone."

Both Rosemarie and Mae nodded their agreement. I waited a little nervously to gauge their reactions. However, their expressions remained impressed, and I didn't observe even the smallest flicker of disapproval.

"Well, I'm off to take a shower. Between those stairs and that spin class, I'm sure I stink." Jill waved, and then bounced off, curly blond ponytail swinging.

Tall, slim Rosemarie tugged her sweatshirt sleeves over her hands and smiled at me shyly. "My brother Matt owns the coffee shop. He told me you'd be working there."

"Of course! I forgot that he said his sister lived here." I felt stupid for not remembering. "I stopped there earlier. He seems like a really good guy."

"He is. We've always been pretty close. I'm glad you're going to work for him. Finding trained baristas in Birch Springs is always a bit of a challenge."

Rosemarie checked her watch. "I'd better head down and give Rosa a hand with supper."

She loped out of the room with a surprising grace, and I was left with the boxes and the petite redhead.

"Do you want a hand unpacking, or would you rather do it alone?" Mae offered.

Honestly, I was a bit overwhelmed. This level of friendly involvement from near strangers made me a bit uncomfortable. The girls had been perfectly nice, and Rosa had made sure I was welcomed. Yet, when I'd moved to Oregon, it had been almost a week before I'd introduced myself to anyone. My first day in town, I'd carried my own boxes into my studio apartment before going off in search of a greasy fast food supper. I wasn't quite sure what to do with so much attention.

"I don't have much. I think I'll take care of it myself," I answered, deciding on the spot to at least attempt to keep some space.

This didn't seem to bother Mae. "Sure. I'm across the hall. We share the bathroom up on this level. I'm sure you'll be able to tell the part of the cupboard I cleared out for you. Holler if you need anything."

I needed no more than forty minutes to put all my things away. Before I let myself sit down, I flattened my trusty boxes and stowed my suitcases for when I would need them next.

I had to admit, the room was very nice. Since I didn't own any furniture of my own, I always had to rent furnished places. Normally, this was a fairly grim arrangement. Sagging beds, decades-old sofas, and mismatched chairs were old friends to me. My bedroom at Bumblebee House, though, was something else altogether.

The room was large, with big windows overlooking both the front and back yards. The walls were painted a pale yellow, and there were two large rugs covering the hardwood floors. I was pretty sure that the bedstead was an antique, and I kept running my fingers over the carved wood of the headboard whenever I paused to put my things on one of the end tables flanking it. There was a beautiful, large chest of drawers and an elegant vanity complete with mirror, as well as a small sitting area with an easy chair and a low bookcase.

Mae knocked on the open door just as I was putting the last of my suitcases away.

"I have to say, you might be onto something," she said as she stepped into the room and looked around. "You can sure move into a place quickly."

I laughed. "That's why I do it. I like the idea of being able to carry everything I own with me and being able to leave whenever I want."

The redhead cocked her head and contemplated that. I half expected some disparaging comment, but instead she said, "It's six o'clock. Supper should be ready."

We headed down the stairs.

"Do you all eat together every night?" I wondered.

Mae nodded. "Every night except Sunday. We're on our own on Sundays. We have a rotation for helping Rosa with supper. Depending on our work schedules, we each sign up to help cook and clean up a few times a week. It's all included in the rent," she explained.

When we reached the first floor, I saw that the dining room table was set. My eyebrows lifted at the tablecloth, colorful matching dinnerware, and crystal stemware.

"Rosa is a bit dramatic," Mae whispered. "She has half a dozen sets of dishes, and she loves picking out which one to use every night. She often matches them to the meal she's cooking."

We headed into the kitchen, where we were put to work carrying dishes full of delicious-smelling food through the butler's pantry and into the dining room. Jill joined us, her hair wet from her shower, and we were soon seated around the dining table.

Rosa took her seat at the foot of the table and said, "Let's pray."

The girls all reached out hands, and we bowed our heads. When Rosa said, "Amen," Rosemarie on my left and Mae on my right both gave my hands a shake. I watched Jill and Rosa do the same.

Rosa caught my confusion and smiled apologetically. "I always forget to warn newcomers. We always 'shake the love around' after we pray. It's something my grandmother did, and I just can't seem to stop doing it."

I nodded slowly. Life at Bumblebee House was unlike anything I'd ever experienced.

The talk around the table was light and fun. The women asked me a few questions about where I was from and what my family was like. They were interested to hear all the places I'd lived, but they took the hint when I didn't go into much detail about my family. My tone and short answers communicated clearly that it was a topic I didn't wish to elaborate upon.

I learned long ago that the best way to get the attention off myself was to ask questions of other people. Before the meal was over, I knew that Jill was from Arizona and taught second grade at the local elementary school. Rosemarie was the youngest of three, and her oldest brother operated their family's ranch just west of town. She and Mae had been roommates in college. When a job opened up at a small outdoor equipment company, Rosemarie had mentioned the job to Mae, who had enthusiastically applied.

The conversation swirled around me as we all cleared the table and helped clean the kitchen.

"Tonight's 'Are You the One?'" Mae mentioned, looking sheepish. "It's totally awful, but we all watch it. Well, Rosa is too refined to indulge, but the rest of us never miss an episode. Want to watch with us?"

I hadn't bothered with a TV in my last two apartments. I'd heard other women talking about 'Are

You the One?', but I'd never watched it myself. To be honest, I had exactly zero interest in the show. But the friendly net of conversation over the supper table had snared me, and I found myself agreeing.

"Okay, this is the third episode of the season," Jill explained as we took our seats in the enormous family room.

Rosemarie lifted the lid of a carved chest and pulled out a handmade afghan. "You haven't missed much."

"I've never watched before," I admitted.

"It's not complex," Mae said, rolling her eyes. "One guy is chosen to be the hero, and he's supposed to find his dream girl. There are twenty women who start, and they do these various tests to see if they are the one. It's seriously the worst. I love it."

I laughed and settled next to her on the couch. As the opening music came on, I looked around at my new housemates and had to admit that this was a much nicer first night in town than I'd ever experienced before.

3

Believe it or not, "Are You the One?" was not only every bit as bad as Mae had promised, there was even an after-show in which the host sat with the contestants and rehashed what had happened during the episode. I begged off and escaped upstairs. The girls' comments had made the show much more enjoyable than it would otherwise have been, but I had an early morning ahead of me. As I jogged upstairs, hooting came from my housemates, and I grinned. They were a fun group.

My alarm went off at 5:30 a.m. and I rolled out of bed with my eyes only half-open. I grabbed one of my two pairs of jeans and a new black "Birch Springs Beanery" v-neck t-shirt. By the time I had shoes on my feet and my hair up in a bun on top of my head, I was at least awake enough to stumble downstairs without doing myself bodily harm.

There was a bowl of fruit on the kitchen island and granola bars in the pantry. I didn't bother to make myself coffee, since I was headed to a café. Besides, I had a feeling that Matt's setup far exceeded anything even Rosa could put together.

I was prepared to open the store but also relieved to see my boss pull in at the same time I did. We were both a bit groggy still, so we worked in tandem turning on machines and making sure everything was ready for the day without much conversation. Matt chose the brew of the day and talked me through more of the day-to-day details once we each had a cup of hot, sweet caffeine in our hands.

Saying that we had a morning "rush" might be a bit optimistic. Still, things stayed steady until around 9:30. By that point, I felt that I had a firm grip on how this coffee shop operated. I'd met many of my new neighbors in Birch Springs. Matt insisted I help myself to coffee whenever I needed it, so I was feeling pretty good when the bell on the door jingled and I looked up, my smile of welcome freezing on my lips.

Nate Weisert sauntered to the counter and leaned on it. "Hello, Emily. See, I remembered your name."

I raised an eyebrow and swallowed the juvenile response of *So? What do you want, a medal?*

Instead, I said, "How can I help you today?"

"Depends on what you're offering?" His beautiful sea-green eyes lit up with anticipation of coming flirtations.

"Coffee," I replied shortly. "What do you want off the menu?" I jerked a thumb at the board hanging behind me.

Nate actually looked disappointed. He straightened and gave me his order, which I rang up as efficiently as possible. As I made his drink, I felt his eyes following my every move, and I was glad that I wasn't someone who blushed easily. Because no matter how much I disliked the way Nate acted, I surely liked the way he looked. Having his attention was flattering, even though I knew he likely gave it liberally to any girl who crossed his path.

I handed the drink across the counter, realized I was too far for him to reach, took a step closer, and managed to skid on a damp patch on the floor. Frantically, I tried to stay upright. My free hand grabbed for the edge of the counter, and the hand holding the cup held on, trying not to drop it. While I was generally successful, I unfortunately sloshed the cup's contents all over my arm and onto Nate as he reached forward in an attempt to keep me from falling.

"I'm so sorry," I apologized automatically the moment my feet were both on dry ground.

"It's fine," Nate crooned.

"You're not burned, are you?" I was picturing the horrible image of causing a lawsuit-worthy scene on my first morning at a new job.

Nate held up his damp arm and grinned. "Nope. No

harm done. I might go and wash up, though, if you don't mind."

"Of course. I'll get you a new drink." I went to the sink and mopped myself up, feeling like a prize idiot. Of all the people to do something stupid in front of!

I made his drink and mopped up the mess before he returned, whistling cheerfully. This time, I handed it over without any disaster befalling me.

"I'm really sorry," I apologized again for good measure.

"Hey, Emily?" He paused until I stopped moving and gave him my full attention. Then Nate smiled and said, "It's really okay."

I let out the breath I'd been holding and scratched my forehead, smiling ruefully.

Nate winked at me, and then whistled his way out the door. I watched him go, and I would be lying if I didn't admit that he was as easy on the eyes going as he was coming.

"Well, I got my first big boo-boo out of the way," I reassured myself. Sure, I would have preferred not messing up in front of Nate, but it wasn't that big of a deal. He wasn't hurt and had taken the whole thing in stride. In fact, he'd been a good sport. I wasn't ready to change my opinion of him, but I did have to give him some credit there.

ONE THING I always try to do wherever I stay for any period of time is to find a way to give back to the community. I've served in soup kitchens, read to senior citizens, and planted trees. The notice board in the Beanery advertised a few interesting options.

On my break, I called the one that stood out to me. Dave at Just Horsing Around was enthusiastic about their summer program for kids with special needs. He suggested that I drop by his office after work and fill out the application to be a volunteer. I would need a background check and some training, but I hung up feeling confident that I'd be spending some time around kids and horses that summer.

It was exactly a week later, in fact, that I found myself climbing out of my van for my first day of volunteering. I'd never been on a ranch before, and I walked around the Triple Star Ranch feeling a bit intimidated. It was quite an operation. The ranch did more than just raise cattle, I had learned from Rosemarie, whose family actually owned the place. Triple Star also had a lodge and conference center where groups could come and stay for retreats or team building. The ranch ran summer programs for kids of all ages, too.

Dave waved me over to the barn, which was covered in childlike paintings.

"Good to see you, Emily," he greeted me. Dave was tall, middle-aged, and balding. From our interview and training time, I also knew him to be very kind-hearted and concerned for the children in his program. "Let me introduce you to our full-time staff. This is Jake, over there is Sarah, and that's Chloe."

I exchanged nods with the other three, who ranged in age from late high school to early 30s.

"During the summer, they're out here each day with the various groups who are bussed in from all over the region. Our volunteers change depending on the day, but these three are always here," Dave explained as we walked through the barn.

I noticed that the interior was handicap-accessible and clearly created for kids. There were boys' and girls' bathrooms, a set of half-circle seating on risers, and everything was colorful.

There wasn't time to get to know the others before Dave brought us together. He ran through the agenda for the afternoon session and gave us a rundown of the special needs we'd be working with specifically. There were to be a fair number of adult volunteers with this group, and so we would be making sure that everything ran smoothly. I learned that Jake worked with the horses and stable hands, Sarah dealt with kids who were too scared to go near horses, and Chloe oversaw each group's riding time.

I was listening intently and nodding along when a newcomer entered through the wide barn door and strode over to the group. It wasn't until he was close to us that I realized anyone was there.

"Sorry I'm late," Nate Weisert said with an aren't-I-a-scamp smile.

I was secretly pleased when Dave frowned at him before continuing with his talk. There was no good reason for me to take so much enjoyment from watching Nate not be adored, but there it was. It particularly chafed me that he was a volunteer here, too. Somehow, working with special needs kids didn't fit with my observations of him, and I wasn't sure that I wanted to give up my superior disdain.

"Emily, will you help everyone get seated once the bus arrives? There are extra chairs in that storage room if the risers don't work for anyone." Dave's eyes met mine only long enough for me to nod before making the next assignment.

Then the sound of the bus pulling to a stop pushed us to action. I watched Chloe and Sarah welcome the group, answer any questions the adults had, and send everyone in to me. The noisy, chattering, wiggly group needed some extra time to get settled, though I had to admit that the kids were extremely cute. Their parents seemed nervous but hopeful that this would be a fun outing.

Once everyone was settled, Dave gave an official welcome, and then called for Jake to bring in the first horse. At the sight of the big creature, the gathered group burst into noise again.

I'd sat next to a little boy named Carlos whose mother didn't appear to speak much English. Carlos had a deep scar on his head and walked stiffly, but he had a huge amount of enthusiasm for the horse.

"Oh, my goodness! Oh, my goodness!" the little boy kept exclaiming as he rocked in his seat, chubby finger pointing at the big animal.

I exchanged a smile with his mother.

Jake talked to the group about riding horses and staying safe in the barn. He had a fabulous way of connecting to the kids without talking down to them.

I glanced at the faces of the children and my eyes caught Nate's, who gave me a little wave. I set aside my automatic annoyance and tried on a friendly smile instead. After all, he was a volunteer with this group. Maybe I'd misjudged him just a tad.

"Are you ready to go outside and ride some horses?" Jake finally said and was met with a rousing cheer.

All the children who could walk on their own got to their feet and followed Chloe out the door.

"Are you coming?" Carlos' little voice grabbed my attention.

I looked down to where he was standing, eyes twinkling, hand held out to me. My heart melted a little, and I said, "You bet!"

The next two hours were filled with helping the group to ride horses around a paddock. The parents walked next to their children as they rode. One girl with cerebral palsy eagerly climbed into the saddle, helmet in place, and beamed out at the world as she rode. A little boy was too afraid, so Sarah took him and his mother to a corral, where he could be near a horse and work up the courage to touch its velvety nose.

I helped out wherever I was needed and mostly avoided Nate, though I will confess that my eyes were drawn to him more often than I cared to admit. By the time the bus pulled away down the long drive and I turned to find him standing next to me, my iciness toward him had thawed a little.

"Nate, show Emily the routine for closing up the kids' barn," Dave ordered.

As we swept up, I tried to find a friendly conversation starter.

"How long have you been volunteering here?" I asked. It seemed like an innocuous topic.

However, my cleaning buddy suddenly looked uncomfortable. Why?

Nate took a few more swipes with his push broom before sighing. "I'm actually not a volunteer, technically."

I stopped my sweeping and cocked my head. This should be interesting.

"I'm doing community service hours."

"Like, for a class or something?" I queried.

Nate shook his head sheepishly. "It's court-ordered."

Disappointment plastered my face. Apparently, Nate Weisert was exactly who I thought he was.

"WHAT?" Nate asked. His lovely sea-green eyes were wide and innocent.

I clenched my teeth and tried not to tell him exactly what I thought of him. *It doesn't matter. You won't know him that long,* I coached myself.

"Look, I'm just disappointed." I looked him directly in the eyes. I'm usually pretty good at honesty, and the least I could do was be straightforward with Nate. Probably part of his problem was that women weren't direct with him often enough. Game-playing of any kind was not my style, though I'll admit that I felt a bit self-righteous at that moment.

His lip curled. "Disappointed?"

"Yep. I was impressed that you volunteered with special needs kids. But doing it just because you're trying to avoid jail time is less impressive." That was putting it mildly.

Nate laughed, but I could see that my words bothered him. "Lucky for me, I'm not trying to impress you."

"Lucky," I repeated with an eyebrow cocked and went back to sweeping.

It wasn't long before he had his cell phone out and was swiping away at something, broom forgotten beside him. I finished the floor, put away the chairs, and cleaned the bathrooms on my own while Nate busily tapped away on his phone. By the time I climbed into my car, I was more than disappointed. I was disgusted.

"Don't forget the team meeting Wednesday night," Doug called before I left.

I waved to him and then drove away. Thoughts of Nate made me angry almost all the way back to town. It wasn't until I slowed toward Main Street that I was able to call up memories of the kids I'd worked with that day. The kids and their parents had been fantastic. Nate aside, I was glad that I'd volunteered. It had been a very good decision.

When I got home, I found Mae in her room, country music blaring. She danced by the door, carrying a stack of folded laundry.

"Oh, hey there, Emily! Is my music too loud? I can totally turn it down if it's bugging you." She smiled, big green eyes crinkling at the corners.

"No, it's fine." I sauntered into the room a little further.

Mae's room was the same size as mine, but with one big addition—the top of the tower was part of her room. It gave her an extra round room with tons of windows. There was a neat little seating area there, as well as a wall of shelves which were filled with all kinds of books.

"Do you like to read?" Mae asked when she noticed me perusing her collection.

I shrugged. "It depends. I like mysteries a lot."

"I love to read," said Mae with a bit of a blush. "I can't help collecting books. There's a big Friends of the Library book sale in Jackson a couple of times a year. Rosa goes to every one, and I always tag along. You know she's the town librarian, right?"

"I think I heard that. Birch Springs can't have a very big library, though, can it?"

"It's in an old storefront downtown. Rosa's done a great job of keeping the old charm while still fighting to make it up-to-date. It's a part of the county system, so she gets people from all over. A lot of other libraries in the area have folded, but Rosa is determined to keep ours open." Mae folded herself into one of the flowered armchairs.

I sank into the one next to her and looked out at the view of the front yard. "This is a really great spot to read. The light is amazing."

"I know. I love it. Whenever I drive past a used bookstore, I always stop now, since I have the perfect place to read. It's like I owe this room, and Bumblebee House, a good book collection up here."

We chuckled.

I looked over her volumes and mused, "When I was at school in Michigan, there was this one enormous used bookstore near Detroit that I visited. This guy took over an old glove factory and put his personal collection in, and then opened shop. It was amazing. Oh, and in Oregon, there's this company of book shops called Smiths. They have a few shops in different towns. I could get lost there forever. They're great, because they just have stacks of books everywhere."

Mae was giving me an appraising look. "I think you are a book lover, Emily McBride, whatever you might say to the contrary."

"You caught me," I said with a grin. "But I use libraries more than anything else. I only carry my absolute favorite books with me."

"I think it's neat that you're so dedicated to having such few possessions. What a great way to keep from getting caught up in capitalism. I can just picture you driving around with one of those tiny houses."

"Right? I would love that. If only I had the money to buy a truck and build one of those suckers." I sighed wistfully.

Mae fiddled with the tassel on the chair's arm. "Does it ever get lonely?"

"Does what get lonely?" I asked, pretending not to understand.

"I just think that never staying anywhere for long must be hard sometimes. I mean, the fresh start would probably feel good, but you're the only one who holds your memories. I guess that's what I like about social media. I'm connected to people who know me and remember the things we've shared." Mae smiled sheepishly. "Does that sound dumb?"

In an uncharacteristic move, I opened the door to my heart the tiniest crack. "No, it makes sense. It is lonely sometimes. My mom and my brother died in a car accident when I was eight. It was just me and my dad after that. Dad was in the Army, and we moved around a lot. He was always busy and didn't spend a lot of time with me. I think I was just a reminder of what he'd lost when Mom died."

"Oh, Emily, that's awful," whispered Mae. "I hate that you had to go through so much, so young."

I looked up and savored her words. They meant more to me than when people just said they were sorry for my loss. "Thank you," I said earnestly. "I guess I don't really know how to keep ahold of people. It's lonely at times, but it's safe. No ties means no obligations."

"Family can be complicated," the petite redhead admitted. "But they can also be really great. Where's your dad now?"

"Denver. He retired from the Army last year and settled in Denver. I think he's working for a security company. I call him whenever I move somewhere new, so he knows how to get ahold of me." I really didn't like talking about my dad. It was time to change the subject. "Where is your family?"

"Oh, that's an interesting story," Mae said and sat up straighter. "My parents are missionaries in Colombia."

"Wait, what?"

"Yeah, I know. I grew up in Colombia, actually. Well, we were in Costa Rica until I was ten, then we moved to Colombia. I came back to the States for college. My sister, Daisy, is nineteen and in her second year at Boise State. She comes to stay here on vacations, usually, though she got a job and an apartment in Boise for the summer."

"Wow, how cool. How did you end up here in Birch Springs?"

"I took a job at Red River Equipment, whose headquarters is outside of town. Actually, I went to school with Rosemarie. She was a couple of years ahead of me, but we were roommates for a while in this really nasty apartment. She knows how much I love the outdoors, and when she heard Red River was opening here, she called me."

"Gotcha. How do you like the job? Have you been there long?"

Mae shrugged. "About three months now. I like it a lot. My boss is great." Her eyes definitely turned a little dreamy, and her fair skin flushed.

Ah, so Mae felt more for her boss than an employee normally did. I was instantly curious about him.

"How's it going at the Beanery? Oh, and how was volunteering?" Mae changed the subject and I followed her lead, not one to push on personal topics.

"The coffee shop is really good. Matt's an easy guy to work for so far. Even Sophie is fun, for a high schooler."

Mae laughed.

"Volunteering was great, too. I loved the kids who were there today. They were so cute up on horses. It was awesome. The staff is so good at dealing with their special needs. Well, most of the staff, that is." I frowned, remembering Nate.

"Uh-oh. What happened?" inquired Mae.

I rolled my eyes. "There's this guy, Nate, who keeps showing up at the Beanery and acting really flirty, which I hate. Flirting is so… fake. I'd far prefer having a normal conversation any day. Anyway, then he turns up at the ranch, and I started thinking that I was wrong to be so annoyed at him. I mean, clearly, he's an upstanding guy if he works with those kids."

"Right," Mae prompted. "Something tells me he's not, though."

"No!" I exploded. "He's only there because it's court-ordered community service. And he left me to do most of the cleanup on my own when he realized I wasn't going to flirt with him. I can't stand him!"

Mae grimaced. "Ouch. That would drive me crazy, too. Well, look on the bright side. Maybe his hours will be finished soon, and he won't be there anymore."

She was right. I could hope that his time was coming to an end. And Nate was not the kind of guy to volunteer once it was no longer required of him, so our hours together were probably limited. It was something hopeful, at least.

Mae was on supper duty and, since I had nothing more pressing to do, I offered to help. We trouped down to the kitchen, where Rosa was gathering ingredients. The three of us got to chopping and simmering ingredients for what Rosa called an "Italian Extravaganza."

As we talked and laughed, I felt my tension over Nate ease away. In fact, by the time we sat down to supper, I was in a very good mood.

"Let's go to the Dairy Treat and get ice cream before 'Are You the One?' starts," Jill suggested.

We all agreed before separating to put on walking shoes and grab our wallets. Birch Springs was small enough that walking anywhere was a manageable task. Lucky for us, the Dairy Treat was on our side of Main Street. The little ice cream novelty shop was open, I learned, from Memorial Day to Labor Day and staffed by local high schoolers. Apparently, it was a popular spot. There were a lot of people in line or making good use of the weather-worn picnic tables.

Though many people called greetings to Rosa or the other girls, we ordered our ice cream and then didn't linger. We strolled back to Bumblebee House, licking away at our melting cones.

It was my third time watching "Are You the One?" and I had developed definite opinions about the various contestants. We all agreed that Kaci was the worst and were vocal about sending her home. However, Jill and I thought Tara was the best choice to marry Garrett, while Rosemarie and Mae were rooting for Hannah.

We all groaned when Julie was sent home instead of Kaci. Rosa padded past and laughed at us.

"You are all far too invested in that fake show," she teased.

"None of us deny it," Jill quipped. "We can handle the truth about our dysfunction."

Mae and I headed up to the third floor and said goodnight after working out our bathroom schedule for the evening and next morning.

As I crawled under the covers, a borrowed paperback Victorian mystery in my hand, I smiled softly. This was more interaction with roommates than I'd ever had before. I had to admit that Mae was right about my life being lonely. I just hadn't realized it before I had such good friends in my life.

5

My schedule at the Beanery varied some, but it was starting to be the sort of thing I could depend on. Sophie was out of school, and so she was able to work any shift, though Matt never wanted her there all on her own for more than a few minutes. After getting to know our lovable-but-somewhat-scatterbrained, part-time gal, I had to agree with him on that one. We were busiest between six and nine in the morning and three and eight at night. Apparently, the Beanery was the cool place to hang out if you were in high school, and so we caffeinated the bulk of Birch Springs' youth and sent them home. Therefore, Matt and I shared opening and closing, with me opening most of the time and Matt handling more evening shifts.

This left me free to volunteer at the ranch two afternoons a week and attend the almost-mandatory staff meetings on Wednesday evenings, which also happened to take place in the Beanery. There was a convenient nook with a big table and benches on three sides, which could be reserved by groups who wanted somewhere to meet.

Dave and the other Just Horsing Around crew had welcomed me right in. Though he was supposed to attend the meetings, Nate had so far only made it to one. On the one hand, I found this very annoying. On the other hand, I was able to relax and enjoy getting to know everyone else without him there to make me feel agitated. I wasn't sure which way was better, but I was certainly good at being annoyed with Nate, no matter what he did.

"It's time for our annual fundraiser," Dave announced at my third meeting.

We were all still settling in with our steaming cups and pens and notebooks. I leaned back, blew on my cup of green tea, and waited.

"Last year we sold chocolate, and that was moderately successful. However, we have a big deficit this year and we really need some more funds to move forward. Triple Star is always very generous with letting us use their facility for minimal costs, of course, but we have other costs, particularly since we try to never refuse a child who wants to be a part of our program." Dave sighed, and I exchanged a look with Jake, who sat across from me. Was Dave worried?

"What have been your most successful fundraisers

in the past?" I asked tentatively, wanting desperately to contribute something to the conversation.

"We've done a lot of different things," Chloe began. "We've sold just about everything you can think of—t-shirts, mugs, chocolate, coffee, gift cards."

Sarah nodded. "Having an event tends to work best, but they take so much work that we often don't have time to make them happen."

It was just then that the door opened and Nate hurried in, as though he was trying his darnedest to get to our meeting. I suppressed my eye roll. Barely.

"Sorry I'm late," he said with a grin, and then nudged me to slide over.

I glared at him and moved into the corner of the booth, making every effort to keep a healthy distance between us.

"What are we talking about?" Nate asked.

Dave caught him up on our fund-raising discussion. I shot Jake an annoyed glance, and he shook his head empathetically.

"I think we should totally just talk to everyone in town and ask for donations," Nate said as soon as Dave finished.

Crickets chirped.

"The trouble is that we would have to make time to meet with everyone in town," I explained, a bit condescendingly if I had to be honest. I cleared my throat and adjusted my tone. "Although asking for donations could be a good way to get ongoing support. There are a number of businesses here in town, and they might have money to use for charitable giving."

The heads around the table bobbed in agreement. Nate sat back in his seat as though he'd contributed all he planned to. I ground my teeth.

"What if we did a talent night here? We could ask locals to come and sing or whatever. We could sell tickets, and I bet Matt would donate part of the proceeds from coffee sales." I stumbled to a stop, trying to rein in my brainstorm.

Everyone else looked a bit skeptical.

It was Chloe who finally said, "A talent show could be really good, but it would be a huge amount of work. I don't know that any of us can take on such a big project right now."

"I can do it," I heard myself offering. Once I realized what I'd just volunteered to do, I gulped.

The eyes of those in my booth lit up.

"Wow, that's really great, Emily!"

"That would be amazing!"

"Let us know how we can help," Dave said, and I noticed that he looked decidedly relieved.

I determined then and there to do my best to make this fundraiser a huge success. Sure, I wasn't a real "joiner" most of the time. I liked to stick to the edges of a crowd and avoid actual commitment. But these special kids needed me. There was no way I could think of little Carlos holding his hand out to me and not give everything I had to raise the money to keep Just Horsing Around running.

We began to brainstorm all we'd need to do to make the event successful. It took awhile to figure out the best date. The Fourth of July was just around the corner, and lots of people traveled during the summer. We argued over several dates but finally decided to hold the show on a Friday night, four weeks away.

Then we got down to the business of logistics.

"I'll design a poster," Jake said as he reached for his ever-present sketchbook.

"Ernie at the print shop in Melbourne is my cousin," Sarah said eagerly. "I'll call him and see if he'll give us some fliers for free."

"I can go around and hand out fliers to all the business in town," offered Nate.

We all blinked at him, pens frozen. After the first week of watching him not help, I'd come to learn that Nate Weisert was really good at avoiding anything that resembled work. He was great with the kids, but never followed through on any task he was assigned.

"Emily, why don't you help Nate? That's going to be a big job," Dave said, nudging me with his eyebrows.

I was instantly annoyed. Why me? Still, I attempted to force a smile and said, "Sure."

"Awesome! The Dynamic Duo!" Nate turned and offered me a high-five.

It would be rude to keep him hanging, so I lifted my hand and slapped his unenthusiastically.

"Listen, I've got to run," Nate said suddenly. "Other plans, you know. So, Emily, you'll let me know when the fliers are ready?"

Typical. "Sure," I replied hollowly.

"Great. See you!" Nate slid out of the booth, and then went to order himself a cup of coffee before he left.

I turned back to the group in time to see Chloe roll her eyes in Nate's direction. At least I wasn't the only one who found his behavior unacceptable.

We were there another hour after Nate's early departure. By the time we got to our feet, we had list upon list of ideas and things to do. I had a master list of everyone's responsibilities, and we agreed on goals that needed to be reached by the following Wednesday night meeting.

I saw that Matt was busy with customers, so I decided to wait until the following day to talk to him about hosting the fundraiser. The sun was down, but the air was still warm and friendly. In a little town like Birch Springs, walking home after dark was not something anyone gave a second thought to. As I strode along, I had to admit that I really appreciated that about this town.

When I finally climbed the steps to Bumblebee House, I could hear music pumping from inside. There was light pouring from every window downstairs. It sounded like a party was going on.

No sooner had I stepped into the wide foyer than I

saw that all the noise was coming from the dining room to my right. I dropped my bag on a bench inside the front door and kicked off my shoes before sauntering in to see what was going on.

Jill and Rosemarie were dancing and singing along to an old pop song on a radio they'd propped up on a chair. There was an enormous mound of clothes covering the top of the dining table.

I stood in the doorway, wondering what in the world was going on.

"Oh!" Rosemarie looked my way and stopped dancing suddenly.

Jill bumped into her and then spun to look at me, her face reddening. "We probably look like lunatics right about now."

I grinned.

Jill scuffled over to the radio and turned the volume down to a normal decibel. "So, I really, really hate doing laundry. Once a month, when I've run out of clean clothes, Rosemarie and I do a billion loads of laundry, and then we have a folding party. It helps me hate it less." Jill watched me, waiting, I'm sure, for some sort of reprimand.

"Do you want another set of hands? I like folding laundry," I offered, then shook my head. Who was it that had taken over my mouth? I kept volunteering for things left and right tonight.

Jill's eyes lit up. "That would be great! Thanks, Emily!" Then she twisted the dial again, and the music filled the room with a pumping beat. "Let's rock and fold!"

Rosemarie groaned at the dorky pun. I just laughed and reached for a pair of pants.

In all fairness, it was an obscene amount of laundry. Jill owned more clothes than most stores, and she had washed them all. With three of us working, it took a full half-hour to fold everything. Granted, Jill wasn't a lot of help. She kept moaning about how much she hated this chore and being distracted by her "favorite" song which was, apparently, all of them. She spent more time dancing and singing than folding, which was fine by me, since it was a very entertaining show. Rosemarie vacillated between singing along and scolding her friend for not doing more.

Finally, we toted all of the stacks upstairs, and Rosemarie and I stood guard as Jill put everything away, complaining the entire time. Of course, the instant the last item was tucked neatly into a drawer, her face lit up.

"That wasn't so bad! Let's go celebrate with ice cream."

Which was how Mae and Rosa, returning from a shopping trip to nearby Clarkston, found us eating Ben and Jerry's out of the container around the kitchen island and giggling about "Are You the One?".

"This sounds like serious girl talk," Rosa teased as she bustled in, looking adorable as always in her vintage 50s dress and matching teal heels.

"I'll have you know, we spent hours and hours doing laundry today," Jill responded, pretending to be outraged.

Mae rolled her eyes and laughed. "We all know what that means, Jill."

"Yeah, I did all the work and Jill did all the avoiding," Rosemarie quipped. "At least Emily was there to save me."

Rosa and Mae leaned against the counter.

"Hey, we're going to be doing a talent show fundraiser for Just Horsing Around," I announced. "Do any of you want to help?"

"A talent show? Fun!"

"Of course we'll help."

"What do you need?"

I grinned around at my housemates. They were an amazing group of women, there was no doubt about that. It would be surprisingly difficult to leave them behind when I moved on. For the first time ever, the thought of moving on made me depressed. What was happening to me?

6

IF I WASN'T sure before, it became apparent that my housemates were some of the best people on the planet. They eagerly asked for details of the fundraiser and jumped in to volunteer for jobs before I even asked. Rosa had a long list of people to contact about performing in the talent show. Rosemarie offered to help waitress and assured me that her brother would definitely be willing to host and contribute part of the proceeds. Mae said she'd talk to her boss about making a donation and promptly blushed furiously. Jill promised to take fliers to school and spread the word to the summer staff.

I went to bed feeling warm and so very grateful. And conflicted. It was becoming increasingly difficult to keep space between me and the people around me. The Bumblebee girls and I had long since passed from acquaintances to genuine friends. This was new and uncertain ground for me, and I wasn't sure what to do about it. Of course, I'd only lived in Birch Springs for a month. It was still the honeymoon phase. Just give it a few months, I assured myself, and you'll be looking for your next adventure.

I didn't have to go in to work until noon the next day, and I took full advantage of my morning off. I didn't set an alarm and slept all the way until 7:30, which for me was sleeping late. I tied on my shoes and went for a long run, then took a refreshing shower and did a load of laundry.

When I sauntered into the Beanery for my shift, my heart was happily thanking God for bringing me to such a good place, though I assured Him that it was temporary.

"Hey there, Em," Matt greeted me when I stepped behind the counter. His gray eyes crinkled at me.

Maybe it was because he was Rosemarie's brother, but I had no ability to see him in any other light. Matt was very good-looking and was normally the sort of guy I would be interested in. I wrinkled my nose as these thoughts flashed through my brain. It felt weird to think about him that way. Maybe it was because he was my boss. Well, whatever the reason, Matthew Donovan was deep in the friend zone.

"Busy day?" I asked as I helped myself to some of the steaming dark roast whose chalkboard sign stated that it was freshly made.

"Not too bad. Rosemarie texted and said you had something to talk to me about. Is it serious?" he asked playfully.

I explained my idea for the fundraiser and our hopes to use the Beanery as the venue. Matt nodded along, listening intently.

"I like it," he announced when I finished talking. "You can definitely have the show here. I'll have to check my figures for the month, but we could probably donate fifty cents of every cup of coffee sold to Just Horsing Around. Maybe you could make a signature drink for the evening."

I grinned at him. "Thanks a million, Matt! Everyone will be thrilled. Do you mind if I call Dave to let him know we're on?"

"Go for it."

He turned to wipe the counter as I pulled out my phone. Soon, Dave was enthusiastically lauding my efforts. Once we hung up, I texted a confirmation of the location to everyone, then put my phone in my back pocket and got to work. Over the next few hours, Jake brought by the sample poster he'd created, and I raved over it.

That evening, Sarah called to tell me she had the fliers printed and wanted to make sure I was still at the Beanery so she could drop them off. After peeking in the box, we both agreed that they were really great, and Sarah beamed at me before trotting out the door. I looked back down at the stack of glossy pages and heaved a sigh. I couldn't put it off any longer.

I texted Nate that the fliers were in and asked when he'd be free to hand them out. An hour later, he texted back with a vague offer to help soon. We wrote back and forth just long enough for my shift to end and for me to be thoroughly annoyed with him. I stomped down the street on the way home, inwardly grousing about irresponsible boys trapped in adult bodies.

Somehow over the next two hours, I managed to pin Nate down, and we agreed to meet the following morning at the café at nine o'clock. I brushed my teeth and readied for bed while numbly listing all the ways that the next day's errand could go horribly wrong, all because of Nate.

My eagerness to prove myself correct meant that I was at the Beanery ten minutes early. Sophie made sure my travel mug was full, and I sat at a table in the front window, scowling at the Nate-free street.

He ambled in fifteen minutes late, which meant that I'd had ten minutes to wait anxiously and fifteen more minutes to grow irritated.

"Hi," he mumbled sleepily. "Let me get some coffee, and then we can get started."

I waited with my foot tapping and my face twisted in annoyed superiority. He returned a few minutes later, blowing on the contents of his plastic cup, and caught my gaze.

"What?" he asked, eyes wide.

I blew out a frustrated breath. "Don't worry about it." While I piously told myself that I didn't want to blast him, I secretly was looking for more things to hold against him. It was entirely childish, I know, but I couldn't seem to help myself where Nate was concerned.

"Where should we start?" I prompted as we stepped out the door.

Nate looked up and down the street and shrugged. "Doesn't matter to me."

I clenched my teeth, then turned and stalked toward the drug store next to the coffee shop. We went inside, me up front and Nate taking his sweet time behind me.

"Hey, Mrs. Davis," he called.

"Is that you, Nate?" an elderly voice answered. "I haven't seen you in such a long time. How's work going?"

I lifted an angry eyebrow. Nate had a job? It was news to me.

He turned on his wide smile and twinkled his sea-green eyes at the white-haired woman behind the counter. "Work is good. Dad's keeping me busy. Say, Mrs. Davis, you wouldn't happen to have any of those peppermints I like so much, would you?"

Mrs. Davis smiled coyly. "Now, Nathan, you know I always keep some behind the counter. Help yourself." She pulled out a large plastic tub of fat, striped candies.

Nate leaned forward and plucked one from the tub. "These were always my favorites growing up."

"I know," the older woman leaned forward and patted his cheek, "that's why I always have some."

I rolled my eyes discreetly. This was precisely the problem with Nate's defective character. He charmed the women around him, who then treated him as though he was a celebrity.

I cleared my throat. The two of them glanced my way. I held up the fliers significantly, and Nate nodded as though he'd just remembered what we were there for. I rolled my eyes less discreetly that time.

"Say, I'm helping out with the Just Horsing Around program out at the Triple Star Ranch," Nate began.

"Isn't that sweet of you," Mrs. Davis cooed.

It took all my mental strength to keep from hollering that Nate was only helping there because it was court-ordered. But that would derail our visit. So I swallowed the words back and tried to smile. I'm pretty sure I failed.

Nate explained the details of the talent show and asked if he could hang a flier in the window. Of course, Mrs. Davis was only too delighted to acquiesce. She found the tape and had Nate climb up among the display to put the flier in a prominent place, where people on the street could see it.

"That looks lovely," she said as Nate climbed back down.

I couldn't take it anymore and jumped in. "We're

trying to raise a significant portion of the program's operating budget. Can we count on this business to contribute five hundred dollars, or some other amount, to Just Horsing Around?"

Nate's eyes bulged. I held my breath.

Mrs. Davis' forehead wrinkled. "I'll have to talk to Mr. Davis, dear. But we'll help out. You can count on us."

Out on the street, Nate turned to me with admiration in his eyes. "Nicely done, Emily."

I shrugged. "People don't know what you are asking them to do if you don't come right out and ask. They can always say no."

We entered the beauty parlor, and it quickly became apparent that Mrs. Davis' treatment of Nate was standard for the town of Birch Springs. He was greeted with cries of delight from both men and women, young and old. The older men would clap him on the back and reminisce about his long-past football glory days. The younger men would laugh raucously and joke about shared memories that always seemed to involve stupid dares. The older women all had kind words, glowing eyes, and little treats for him. The younger women puffed up and preened, slapping at his arm flirtatiously.

After forty minutes, we'd covered half of Main Street, and I'd witnessed the same routine a dozen times. It was astonishing and a little unnerving. No wonder Nate seemed like a high schooler who had never left home. That was the way the entire town treated him!

We walked out of the hardware store where the owner, Bill, and a half-dozen older men in faded overalls had chortled over the way Nate had thrown for over a hundred yards in the "big game." I shook my head. Though they'd allowed us to put up a flier and promised donations, the conversation had mostly revolved around Nate's glory days.

I turned to him, mouth open, to say something, though I wasn't sure what.

Nate was looking at his phone and frowning.

"What's up?" I queried.

He squinted down the street at the rest of the shops. "I didn't really think this would take so long. I've got somewhere I need to be."

"Where do you have to be? You promised to help pass out fliers." I jabbed an accusing finger at him.

"What do you think we've been doing the past hour?" He looked at me as though I was losing my mind.

"'The past hour'? We've only been doing this for a little over half an hour, because you were late." I savored how good it felt to throw that in his face. "If you would stay focused, we could have been done by now. Instead, we have to listen to you flirt with everyone in this town."

Nate's brow dropped. "That's out of line. It's not my

fault that people like me. You probably don't know what that's like. See you later."

I watched him go, speechless. After that, I was too angry to finish passing out fliers. I promised myself I'd do the rest the following day and stalked home, radiating anger and irritation.

Unsurprisingly, Nate stopped responding to my texts the next day as I tried to reschedule a time to finish handing out fliers and asking for donations. After my morning shift, I had to handle the task on my own. I had to admit that Nate had made it look easy the previous day. Where the shopkeepers and business owners welcomed him like a long-lost son, I was greeted with tight-lipped smiles and wary glances.

By the time I finished with the last business on Main Street, I was one big, tangled ball of emotions, none of which were good, and all of which were pointed fiercely at Nate. I was annoyed that he was so dang charming, and I was most definitely not. I was angry that he'd ditched me with the job only half-done. I was worried that the donations I'd attempted to solicit would be much smaller, since Nate hadn't been there to help.

Matt texted later that afternoon to ask if I could close. He was needed at the ranch by his brother. I was happy to step in and lend a hand.

So, I pulled my Beanery v-neck back on, put my hair up in a high bun on the top of my head, and scooted back out the door with a wave to Mae, who was doing some sort of weird yoga in the study.

"Thanks a million for filling in," Matt gushed. "Sophie specifically asked for tonight off, so you were the only person I could call."

I laughed at his concern. "It's really fine. No worries."

He left, still apologizing, and I busied myself washing up a few dishes while the café was empty.

A few customers came and went over the next hour, but things were pretty quiet. I was able to mess around with combinations for my signature drink for the talent show.

Around nine o'clock, the door opened, and I looked up to see Nate stroll in and grin at me as though we were the best of friends. He approached the counter, attention on the menu board. I was sort of impressed that he didn't burst into flames from the evil glare I was spearing him with.

Finally, his eyes met mine and he stepped back a tiny bit. "Whoa. What's that look for?"

I squinted at him. Could he really be this oblivious? "Did you get my texts?"

"Oh, yeah, I did. I forgot to write back and tell you I

was busy." He looked relieved, as though this happened all the time and was no big deal. "Can I get a half-caf latte?"

"Sure," I snarled.

The buffoon didn't seem to notice that I was trying not to throttle him. Not only did he take his drink with a jaunty, "Thanks, Em," but he then proceeded to sit at the table nearest the counter, pull out his phone, and glance at me repeatedly while he sipped his coffee.

I put all my mental energy into ignoring him while I served the group of teenagers who burst through the door, all demanding sugary caffeine. They greeted him like a dear friend, which Nate seemed to enjoy very much. I was glad when it was closing time and I could push them all out the door.

For reasons I can't explain, over the next week, Nate suddenly decided to spend all his free time in the café whenever I was working. No sooner would I start my shift, then he would appear, with the exception of when I opened. In which case, he would appear at ten o'clock without fail and manage to linger for at least an hour.

The only way for me to survive this new habit of his was to keep our interactions short and to the point, and then to ignore him with every fiber of my being.

Therefore, I was irritated with him before I even arrived at the Triple Star Ranch for my next volunteering session. Just knowing that he'd saunter in, late as always, made my eye twitch.

"Oh, I'm glad you're here early," Dave said as soon as I entered the barn. "I wanted to give you the sign-up list for the show."

We discussed the progress we'd made, and I updated the lists in my notebook. Jake, Sarah, and Chloe each came over, and we had an impromptu check-in. Though no one said it, we all knew that it was easier to meet without Nate being there, annoying us all.

Then the bus pulled in and we jumped into action. This group had several wheelchairs, and we would need all hands on deck. Which was made more challenging since Nate was nowhere to be found. The five of us wrestled everyone into place and found chairs for all the parents.

It wasn't until Jake brought out Sparkles the pony that Nate arrived, sunglasses on and dressed like he was trying to impress a country club crowd. Since the rest of us were in our Just Horsing Around polo shirts, old jeans, and dirty boots, Nate only managed to stand out even more than usual.

I exchanged an annoyed glance with Sarah, and then ignored him when he leaned against the wall next to me. Unfortunately, his proximity proved to work against me.

Dave took the floor with his last-minute reminders and began to explain what would happen next. Because of all the kids in wheelchairs, there were fewer kids in the group and more chaperones. This had happened before and I knew that, once the actual interaction with horses began, I might be given an administrative job.

Sure enough, Dave instructed three kids and their parents to go with Sarah and the other two to go with Chloe. I helped everyone get out the door. Then Dave turned to me and said, "Why don't you and Nate go into the office and make some fundraising calls?"

My smile turned wooden. I mumbled, "Sure." I stomped off toward the office, Nate trailing behind.

Over the next hour and a half, I left six voicemails, confirmed five donations, got another dozen promises, and emailed the dress rehearsal schedule to the participants in the talent show. Nate made two calls and scrolled on his phone. I tried to pretend that he wasn't there, but every time I looked his direction and saw him avoiding helping with this very important cause, my blood pressure rose a little more.

Dave came in as I was finishing the last call on my list. "How's it going?" he asked.

"Pretty good," Nate answered for me. He reached over and picked up my list of calls and handed it to Dave.

"Looks like you two made great progress."

"Thanks," said Nate.

Luckily, Dave checked his watch, handed my list back, and went back out to the barn before he could get in the splash zone of my fury.

My temper exploded like Mount St. Helens. "I can't believe you," I hissed.

"What?" Nate asked, leaning back in his chair and clicking his pen aimlessly.

"You just sat here doing nothing for an hour and a half, and then took credit for my work! In all my life, I've never met a lazier person than you." I slammed my notebook onto my closed laptop.

Nate blew that off with a shrug. "Whatever."

Even as I continued, I knew my words were needlessly cruel, but I couldn't seem to stop myself from pouring out my long list of complaints against him. "You expect everyone to treat you like the crowned prince, and most people do it. Who cares if you could throw a ball ten years ago? If your best days were in high school, you have a long life of being mediocre ahead of you.

"And the worst thing is that you expect nothing of yourself! You excuse yourself from doing anything worthwhile. The kids who come here benefit tremendously from this program, but the only reason you're here is because you have to be. Then, you shirk your chores and leave more for the rest of us to do."

I was shaking with anger. "Every time I don't treat you like you hung the moon, you look at me like you can't figure out why I haven't fallen for your charms. Maybe no one else has had the decency to tell you the truth, but I will. You are a good-for-nothing, lazy pretty-boy. When I leave this town, you will be the thing I'm happiest to leave behind."

Face stony, Nate got to his feet, fists clenched. "You don't know anything about me," he snarled. "You don't know what my life has been like."

"Maybe not, but I have plenty of behavioral evidence to consider."

"Shut up," he hissed. "You're completely wrong."

My eyebrows rose up in challenge. "Am I? Go ahead and prove me wrong. I would love it if you got yourself together and showed me that you do care about something other than yourself. These kids would be a fantastic place to start. Oh, wait, you're only here working with these kids with special needs because you're trying to avoid going to jail. Huh. I think that proves my point."

Nate looked like he was caught between fury, humiliation, and the need to punch something.

"It's not like you have your life all together," he flung out desperately.

"I'm not saying I do. It doesn't matter if I have my life together, I'm making a difference. I care about other people. You, however, are completely self-absorbed. The only time you look around at other people is when you want something from them. You want the attention of some pretty girl, or you want someone to give you attention." My initial temper was cooling, and I found myself wanting to tell him the truth rather than to hurt him. Mostly.

"I actually liked you." Nate stood with his hands on his hips, looking betrayed.

"What did you like about me? How I look? What I can do for you? You say that you liked me, but you never once tried to be my friend. All of our interactions have been about you trying to get me to do whatever it is that you want. You could have talked to me instead of hitting on me. You could have seen when I needed help and pitched in. But you didn't. Not once." I crossed my arms, feeling like I'd just won my case.

Nate stood still for a long moment before turning and walking out the door without another word. I stepped to the window and watched him walk, defeated, to his car. He waved at someone without looking that way. I'd never seen him looking so hurt before.

I spent the rest of that day mulling over the words I'd thrown at Nate. I'd been harsh, hurtful even. I'd said true things, but had I been too cruel? Had my sharp words cut too deeply? I swung between feeling like my words were justified and berating myself for being unkind.

I expected to see him at the Beanery over the next few days, but he didn't show up. He wasn't at our Wednesday night staff meeting for Just Horsing Around, either. Dave mentioned that Nate had texted to say he'd be absent. Guilt wrapped itself around me, and my face grew hot.

What had I done?

8

As I DROVE the six miles to the ranch for my next afternoon of helping kids, I actually hoped Nate would be there. Historically, I had few qualms about telling people things that other people couldn't or wouldn't. I figured that since I wouldn't be anywhere for long, it didn't matter if my honesty affected our relationship.

Maybe it was Birch Springs itself that was making me need to know if Nate was okay. The sweet little town was growing on me more and more each day, and I actually found myself delaying thoughts of moving on whenever they'd pop up. Of course, my friends at Bumblebee House were also braiding our lives together, and I wondered if I would be able to extricate myself without inflicting serious pain on someone.

I refused to believe that my concern was due to anything about Nate himself. I found him irritating, immature, and totally self-centered. Sure, he was very good-looking and far more charming than anyone had a right to be. But I didn't like him. At all. Right?

To my very great surprise, Nate's souped-up Jeep was already parked near the barn when I arrived. I frowned at it as I pushed my sunglasses up and strode past. Nate never got anywhere early.

I entered the barn and stopped in my tracks. He was putting out folding chairs. My eyebrows were one with my hairline.

Jake walked in just after I did and said, "I'm guessing aliens."

"Huh?" I asked.

"Aliens. I think he was abducted, and some alien took over his brain. He's probably here doing recon for some lost tribe from Mars or something."

I grinned at Jake and went to the office to discuss the newest developments with Dave.

All the Just Horsing Around staff watched Nate with disbelief that afternoon. He quietly helped the kids and parents, then went over and above what was asked of him when it was time to tidy up. He didn't say much, and he definitely avoided meeting my eyes. When he waved goodbye and headed off to his car, Sarah and I exchanged wide-eyed looks.

Had my words had such an effect on him? Or was he just trying to prove a point? Surely, this new-and-improved Nate wouldn't stick around for long.

But by Wednesday night's meeting at the Beanery,

Nate 2.0 showed up again. He was early and offered to get napkins for Chloe when her coffee tipped.

"The talent show is a week from Friday, can you believe it?" I asked the group. "We are in good shape, but there's still a lot to be done. Dave, what's the plan for the dress rehearsal?"

Nate's phone pinged, but he didn't reach for it. Instead, he sipped his coffee and nodded along with what Dave was saying. I was impressed.

Matt came over with small sample cups of the signature drink I'd invented. Everyone sipped it thoughtfully and began nodding.

"I wanted it to be a really special drink," I explained. "That's why there's whipped cream on top. And I added the minty chocolate flakes on the whipped cream so it would look like an Appaloosa. I'm calling it an Appaloosa Latte. What do you think? Is it too much?"

The group was quick to assure me they loved the drink, thought it was just right for the event, and they liked the name idea.

I made a check mark on my to-do list next to "create signature drink" with a relieved smile. I'd put a lot of thought into my concoction and would have been secretly crushed if the feedback had been negative.

"How are ticket sales?" I asked.

Chloe began her report. We all nodded along as she spoke. We moved on to talking about all the other pieces that needed to come together to make the event a success. They hadn't been kidding—it was a lot of work. But from what we could tell, we'd be raising several thousand dollars in this one evening.

"Do we have an emcee for the night? Dave, did your friend at the news station ever get back to you?" I asked as we reached the final item on my list.

Dave looked as though he'd been waiting for us to ask him this very question. "Yes, I've been able to confirm that Ted Wilmington will be our emcee."

The rest of us weren't nearly as impressed as he wanted us to be. Dave looked between our faces, read no more than mild satisfaction there, and deflated slightly.

I intervened. "That's fantastic, Dave! A real celebrity. I bet a lot of people will want to come just to see him."

This appeased him slightly, and we were able to wrap up the meeting without any more toes being stepped on. Once the meeting finished, the group was quick to disperse. Soon only Nate and I remained. He helped me return the extra chairs we'd borrowed and wipe down the table.

Nate had been quiet and attentive all night. It was time for me to say something.

"Hey, Nate, I wanted to say thanks for all your hard work lately. We've all appreciated you pitching in," I said, careful to sound casual.

"I'm glad I've been able to help. You all do a lot around the ranch. I should have noticed earlier and made things easier for all of you a long time ago." He seemed genuinely ashamed of himself.

It was exactly what I'd wanted to see just last week. But now, Nate's embarrassment didn't give me any pleasure. To my surprise, I didn't want him humiliated after all. I was glad that he was helping out, sure, but my stomach clenched when I remembered that it was my harsh words that had prompted this action. I wasn't sorry for being honest. However, I knew that hearing the truth had been really hard on him.

"I could use a hand getting decorations from Melbourne, if you have some time to spare," I heard myself offer.

Nate pulled himself out of his self-deprecation a little. "Really? When were you thinking of going?"

"I have Saturday morning off, so I was planning to go then. There's a craft store that has agreed to donate some centerpieces." For reasons I didn't want to examine too closely, I felt a little wobbly as I explained, waiting to hear if Nate would agree to run this errand with me.

"Yeah, I could definitely give you a hand."

And that was how I found myself sitting in my van, Nate Weisert next to me, wound up like a clock. We'd agreed to meet at the Beanery at nine. Since we weren't sure if his Jeep would have enough room for the decorations, we had decided to take my van.

I clutched my travel mug full of Matt's best

Columbian coffee and tried to figure out what to say to break the awkward silence.

Fortunately for me, a great Dolly Parton song came on, and Nate's eyebrow rose.

"I didn't peg you as the country-music type," he said.

I glanced at him and read only interest and no scorn there. So I shrugged and said, "I guess I like a lot of different kinds of music. I tend to like specific artists more than genres. What kind of music do you like?"

"I'm not much of a music guy, actually. I listen to whatever's on the radio, but I don't give it much thought."

When I glanced at him this time, his eyes were apologetic and begging me not to be too hard on him. I sighed heavily.

"Listen, Nate, I need to apologize for how I spoke to you the other day. I think I was way too harsh."

He was quiet for almost a full minute, his eyes searching the distant horizon. Then, tentatively, as though he was feeling out the ice under his feet, he said, "I think I needed to hear you say those things. So don't apologize. If anything, I should apologize to you."

"Still, I shouldn't have been so mean about it. I definitely crossed a line."

Nate reached out a hand and touched my elbow.

At his touch, I almost jerked the steering wheel. I couldn't believe the jolt of electricity that passed between us.

However, if anything had sparked for me, it clearly didn't for Nate, who went on earnestly. "Don't beat yourself up about it, Emily. If you hadn't said it the way you did, it might not have gotten through to me."

It was really kind of him to be so forgiving. For the first time, I felt my heart quivering a little.

"Can you forgive me for how I behaved?" he asked.

"Of course," I stammered.

He gave me a crooked grin. "Thanks. Really, Em, thanks for being so honest with me. Can we be friends?"

"Sure," I whispered, cheeks flushing. Suddenly, being just friends with Nate was disappointing. What was happening to me?

"Okay, if we're going to be friends, we should know each other better. Let's play Twenty Questions."

I laughed. "The only way I've played Twenty Questions is trying to guess something, and I have a feeling that's not what you're talking about."

"Right-o. I mean that we each get to ask the other person twenty questions, and we have to each answer them too. So, if I ask you what your favorite color is, I have to tell you mine, too. It's red, by the way."

I looked over at those sea-green eyes and bright smile and swooned a little. *Get yourself together, girl!* I chastised myself mentally.

"Let's do it. My favorite color is green," I said. "Umm… What was your first pet? Mine was a hamster named Carlos."

"Really? Carlos? How did that happen?" Nate chuckled, and then sipped at his cup, totally at ease.

"My brother named him. I wanted to name the hamster Galadriel, so it probably worked out better that he ended up as Carlos. My brother probably cried until he got his way." The memory made me sad. I'd lost my brother when he was seven. Carlos had been the last pet he'd ever had.

I could feel Nate's eyes on my profile, but I couldn't bring myself to look at him. I really didn't want to talk about David at the moment.

"My first pet was a dog. I think it was a golden retriever-corgi mix. Anyway, her name was Sammy, and I always wanted her to be a show jumper, except that her legs were really short. My older sister, Lucy, would yell at me for trying to make Sammy go over jumps. What is your family like?" he asked his next question.

My stomach clenched. This was always such a tricky question for me. My entire family situation was such a downer that I didn't usually want to talk about it at all, unless I knew the questioner really well. And I rarely let relationships get to the point where that was going to happen.

"It's not a great story," I said and glanced at him to see how that went over.

"Tell me whatever you want. If you don't want to talk about it, you can have a pass on that question."

And, to my surprise, I did want to talk about it. "My

mom and my brother, David, were killed in a car accident when I was eight. It was just me and my dad after that, and he never really got over it. So we aren't very close. I call him when I move to a new place, but we don't talk much. What about your family?"

Nate paused, and I looked over to see him watching me closely. Was he trying to make sure I was okay? My stomach unclenched and my heart sighed.

When he saw that I wasn't going to fall apart, Nate went on to tell me about his parents and older sister, who all still lived in Birch Springs. From there, our question-asking ranged from the practical (what is your shoe size?) to the fantastic (if you could have one superpower, what would it be?). We lost track of the number of questions we'd each asked long before we arrived in Melbourne.

At the store, Nate jumped out of the van and was quick to help load the boxed centerpieces. He insisted we grab lunch, and we laughed and talked the whole time.

By the time we arrived back at the Birch Springs Beanery, we were fast friends. And, to be completely honest, I had developed the start of a serious crush on Nate Weisert. It was ridiculous, since I'd been so disgusted by him only a few weeks earlier. But I was definitely swoony where he was concerned.

9

THAT MONDAY WAS five days before the talent show. I opened the Beanery feeling like all was right in the world. Everything was on schedule, and we were going to raise a lot of money to keep Just Horsing Around operating. As I walked to work in the early morning just-before-dawn, I marveled at how good life was at that moment. I was fully prepared to deal with any little problems that arose. I'd spent the weekend tweaking the centerpieces with Rosa's expert help, and now they were adorable. I'd watched a dumb romantic comedy movie with Jill, who burst into tears at the end even though she'd seen it twice before, and we both had a good laugh at her expense. Mae and Rosemarie had sat on the back porch with me for an hour yesterday, and we'd laughed over our memories of middle school.

But secretly, I knew that the real reason I felt so

rosy that morning was because of Nate. The hours we'd spent together Saturday morning had left me feeling optimistic and cheerful. Even now, days later, I was still walking with a special pep in my step, thanks to that all-too-handsome fellow.

Oh, I'd given myself plenty of scoldings, believe you me. *He is a charmer, no matter what sudden changes he might be showing to you. He's never had a girl who didn't fall for him, you are just one more in a long line. You aren't going to be here long enough for anything to happen, so stop acting so silly!*

I couldn't. I couldn't stop thinking about him and smiling. I couldn't stop looking up hopefully every time the bell on the door jangled at work, in case it was him. And I finally admitted to myself that I'd liked him all along, despite his rude behavior.

My heart soared when he finally walked into the coffee shop around midmorning.

"Hey, pal," he said with a teasing smile as he approached the counter.

"Hey, buddy," I shot back. "What can I get you?"

Nate leaned on the counter and sighed. "If I don't get some major caffeine, I am not going to make it through the rest of this day. I always tell myself, 'today is the day I don't have any coffee,' and then I regret that decision by about 9:15."

I laughed. "I gave up that struggle long ago. Caffeine is here to stay."

"Amen, sister," he said and gave me a high-five.

"What'll it be today? Extra large, five espresso shots?"

"Any chance you could make me one of those special drinks you're going to serve at the talent show?" Nate wheedled.

My cheeks turned pink. "The Appaloosa Latte? You liked that one?"

"Of course I did. It was every good thing in a cup."

I was all too glad to turn away and busy myself making his drink.

"So, do you feel ready for Friday night?" Nate asked.

"Sometimes," I admitted. "Then at other times I remember all we still have to do and feel a bit overwhelmed."

"Let me know if I can help. That sounded flippant." He leaned forward and said quietly, "One of my new resolutions is not to be flippant. So, I'm honestly offering you help with anything."

I felt stunned. He'd made resolutions? I had to shake my head to clear it and say something moderately sensible. "We've got a rehearsal tonight over at the church. If you want to come along, it might be nice to have another set of hands."

"What time?" Nate whipped out his phone, and then looked at me expectantly.

"Seven."

His fingers tapped away. Then he looked up at me, sea-green eyes serious. "Cool, I've got you on my calendar."

I handed his cup over and managed a weak smile.

Nate lifted the drink and grinned. "Thanks! Well, I'd better head back to the office so Dad doesn't send out a search party."

I stood waving numbly a few beats after the door swung closed behind him. Then I looked around to make sure nobody was watching. I grinned at no one for the next five minutes.

As it turned out, we were really glad to have Nate at the rehearsal. I hadn't thought through what we would do when we didn't have our emcee at the practice nights. For a long, awkward minute, I wasn't sure what to do, since both Dave and I were busy with other jobs. Then Nate raised a hand and volunteered to fill in.

Sarah had written a brief introduction for each act. Nate bounded onto the stage and did a fantastic job. He poured all his charm into the intros, and the performers were grinning when they came out to run through their acts.

This was especially helpful because not all of the performances went very well. The magician kept fumbling his cards. The group of local dancing toddlers forgot to dance when the music came on. We couldn't figure out how to get the microphone to work so that the singer could be heard over her guitar playing.

Still, Nate kept us laughing the entire night. I couldn't stop thinking about the change in him as I tried, and failed, to read my mystery before bed. After debating about it for over an hour, I finally texted him to say thanks for helping. He texted back a smiling emoji, and I went to sleep hoping to see him again the next day.

My wish came true. Nate came by every day during his midmorning break. He came to each night's rehearsal and did the job of emceeing every evening. When Friday night rolled around, he was the first to arrive at the Beanery and began taking orders from me even before we closed the café until the event began.

I felt my nerves thrumming as each minute passed. There was so much to do, and I was hyper-focused. If I was barking orders, everyone seemed willing to overlook it.

Finally, at thirty minutes before we were scheduled to begin, the first performers began to arrive, and I stood in indecision near the counter. I scoured my checklist, unwilling to believe that we'd finished every task. But, no, our team was working smoothly. Jake was doing a sound check. Sarah was showing performers to the waiting area at the back of the store. Matt and Sophie were prepping everything for the night's food and drink service. Chloe was instructing the four high school waiters on how they were to serve drinks and keep track of bills. Dave was putting the final touches on his ticket table at the entrance.

Nate appeared at my elbow. "Everything looks great. Except you."

I jerked my head. "Excuse me?"

"You need to go get dressed, Em. People are going to start arriving soon." He was smiling impishly.

A quick scan down at my shorts, flip-flops, and Beanery t-shirt confirmed Nate's evaluation of my appearance. I noticed that he was wearing a dark blue military-style shirt that made him look even better than usual. I gulped, remembering how I looked at that moment, and beat a hasty exit to Matt's office, where the bag with my change of clothes was waiting for me.

I took time in the bathroom, putting on makeup and making sure my hair was just right. As the moving force behind the event, I wanted to look especially good. All right, and I wanted Nate to think I was pretty.

When I emerged, people were starting to arrive. A few were ordering drinks at the counter, others were settling into their chairs and hailing a waiter. Sarah caught my eye and gave me the thumbs-up. I hoped that meant that we weren't missing any performers.

I tried to spot Nate, but a frantically waving Dave drew my attention at the front door. I moved in that direction, trying to look calm and collected.

"I just heard from Ted Wilmington," Dave whispered frantically and held out his phone. "He's not coming!"

I groaned. We'd advertised that Ted Wilmington would be our emcee. It was one of the things that had made our rinky-dink talent show seem more legit. Now we were celebrity-less.

"Nate's been practicing all week. Maybe he'd be willing to step in," Dave suggested.

It wouldn't be the same, but it was our best option.

"I'll go ask him." I offered a brave smile to the elderly couple shuffling in to the shop ahead of me.

Nate was talking to a group of very cute young women. I grabbed his elbow and pulled him away.

"Hey, Em. Wow. You look great." He grinned.

It wasn't exactly the stunned response I'd been dreaming of when I was getting dressed, but the sheen of sweat on my brow surely wasn't doing me any favors.

"Ted Wilmington isn't going to make it," I said without preamble. "Is there any way that you could emcee?"

Nate thought that over, and then shrugged. "Sure, I guess. I don't know if I'm dressed right, though."

I glanced at his khakis and blue shirt. "You look fine."

"Aw, thanks. You're pretty fine yourself." He waggled his eyebrows at me.

I snorted, and then punched him on the arm. "Get serious, you dork." I pulled the emcee notes from the back of my clipboard and handed them over.

He winked at me, made his way to the stage, and began to review the notes we'd been tweaking all week.

The Bumblebee girls arrived and were quick to ask if I needed them to do anything.

"Actually, no, I don't," I said with surprise. "Just buy yourself a drink and enjoy the show."

"Break a leg!" Mae whispered and gave me a quick hug before following the others to join the queue for the counter.

I noticed that Matt and Sophie were looking a bit harried, so I pushed through the crowd, slipped back to the work area, pulled an apron over my head, and dove into the drink-making frenzy.

Promptly at 7:30, Dave stepped up to the microphone and welcomed everyone. "Thank you for coming out and supporting not only our fabulous performers, but also this wonderful program. Just Horsing Around is in its eighth year of serving the special needs community of Western Wyoming." He talked a few more minutes, then wrapped things up with a hearty, "We hope you enjoy the show!"

The polite clapping was spattered with good-natured chuckles as Nate took the stage.

"No, you don't need to get your eyes checked. I am not Ted Wilmington." He grinned at the audience, who laughed at their favorite hometown kid.

The chaos behind the counter ebbed enough for us to catch a few of the acts. I watched our magician with a nervous cringe, but he actually pulled off most of his tricks. The one major fumble he had was handled with humor, and there was tumultuous applause as he bowed.

The dancing toddler group was completely

adorable. All of their parents were in the room, and so there was a veritable wall of phones filming the little girls' every move. One little one cried through the whole performance. Another sat down and played with her shoe rather than join in with the others. Two girls bumped into each other before knocking over a third. All of this just added to the cuteness.

But really, the best act of the night was Nate. He sparkled up on the stage. His charm won over every person in the room. I noticed the table full of his admiring female friends watching his every move. They paused to put on a fresh layer of lip gloss before rushing over to congratulate Nate on the good job he'd done.

I looked down at my stained apron and sighed. Halfway through the night, I'd given up and thrown my hair up into an untidy bun to get it out of my way. I had no doubt that I'd sweated my makeup off long ago. Even though the night had been a success, I couldn't help feeling like the grungy maid.

I pushed the overwhelming feelings of not being good enough aside and forced myself to worry about wrapping the event up well. We had cleanup to do and money to count and a hundred other little things. The Bumblebee girls offered to stay and help us, and I was too tired to refuse.

Finally, with the buzz of success humming around us, I wished my fellow Just Horsing Around friends goodbye and let my housemates take me home to bed.

10

I WENT HOME, changed out of my dress and into my favorite t-shirt and sweats. I was still humming from the long day of emotions and expectations and wasn't ready to sleep, even though it was late. The other Bumblebee girls bid me goodnight and headed off to bed. I put the kettle on in the kitchen and rooted through Rosa's store of tea bags.

Once my cup of mint tea was ready, I padded out to the back porch and settled onto one of the well-cushioned swings. I leaned back, one leg curled under me, the other stretched down to the wooden boards so I could rock gently. The night wrapped around me as I sipped and swung. A chorus of crickets serenaded me. The stars filled the sky. The warm wind stroked my bare arms.

I should have been reveling in the success of the talent show. But I wasn't. I felt all jumbled up inside. To my surprise, tears sprang to my eyes and then spilled over onto my cheeks. I sniffled and tried to take a deep breath.

"What's wrong with me?" I prayed. "Why aren't I happier about tonight?"

I waited for an answer. Images of Matt and Sophie willingly volunteering their time popped into my mind. I pictured the Bumblebee girls, quick to help wherever they were needed. I saw each act flash by, accompanied by the sound of the audience clapping and cheering. There was Nate, stepping in and stealing the show.

And there I was: on the fringe. I'd been an integral part of making the night happen, sure, but I wasn't a permanent part of the picture. This community of friends and neighbors beckoned me like none had done before. A part of me longed to fit into the puzzle of Birch Springs. To truly belong here.

The wind caressed my face, and I thought of my mother. When I got sick as a little girl, Mom would make me a nest on the couch. She would bring me apple juice with a straw and a plate of saltine crackers. She would make sure the TV was at the right angle and volume. She would lean down, kiss my forehead, and gently caress my cheek.

The tears were really falling then. I missed my mother so much in that moment that I thought my heart would burst. Almost twenty years later, I still felt her loss deeply.

After Mom died, sick days had little comfort. Dad was busy at work and let me know that I was being an inconvenience. There was a gaping chasm between us, and we were never able to build a bridge across it. Whichever house or apartment we lived in never felt like home. Home had been my mother, and she was gone.

Maybe that was what was pulling at my heart tonight. For the first time, I had a place in which I could build a home. A real home. One with warmth and memories, love and true friendship.

And that was terrifying to me, because I knew that as good as home was, the loss of it was a terrible thing.

Which was why I finished my tea, crept up to bed, and told myself that I would start looking for the next place to go first thing in the morning. I couldn't risk staying in Birch Springs, in Bumblebee House, any longer.

MATT HAD OFFERED to cover my shift the morning after the talent show. He'd predicted that I'd be wiped out. I'd been too stubborn to let him help me out, and so I was standing, uncharacteristically bleary, behind the counter at six a.m. the next day. I'd even allowed myself to drive to work, which I never did. But the snooze button on my phone had whispered its seductions to me, and I couldn't resist.

There was a steady stream of our regular customers. Each had a word of praise for the talent show. Their kindness poked at the bruise around my heart. I tried to smile each time, reminding myself I'd be leaving soon.

I was at least more awake by midmorning. It didn't hurt that I'd required a second cup of coffee to finally push me out of my bleary funk. I wasn't anywhere close to cheerful, but I was at least able to pretend that everything was fine.

My pretense wobbled severely when the door opened and Nate came in. He waved at me before joining the short line of customers awaiting their Saturday morning caffeine fix. Sophie came in behind Nate, quickly donned an apron. and took over the cash register.

I was able to mostly ignore Nate while he ordered, though I had to hand over his drink. My eyes refused to meet his, so I don't know if he noticed that I wasn't quite myself.

However, when I handed over his cup, his fingers closed over mine. He paused, and my gaze betrayed me, swinging up in surprise and locking with his.

"Can you take a quick break? I wanted to talk to you about something," he asked.

I looked over at Sophie, who hadn't missed anything.

"Take your break. It's cool," she said with a suggestive grin.

I rolled my eyes at her, and she popped her gum in response, wiggling her eyebrows.

The café was mostly empty. The July weather was too beautiful to stay inside. I followed Nate outside to a tall table tucked into an alcove. We climbed up into our seats.

"What's up?" I tried to sound nonchalant. My stomach was quivering, my heart was pounding, and my brain was busy telling them both to stop being ridiculous. We were leaving soon, and they had no reason to act this way.

Nate was unusually serious. He sipped his coffee, took a deep breath, then plunged in. "I know you haven't always liked me too much, but I really like you, Emily. A lot. I didn't handle it well in the beginning." He looked embarrassed and nervous, and my brain stopped lecturing my heart. "I was hoping that you'd go on a date with me." Nate's eyes shyly met mine.

"I'd like that," I answered automatically. I think my heart was eager to keep my brain from having its say.

"Really? Great! What are you doing tonight?"

And before I knew what was happening, I had agreed to let Nate pick me up at eight o'clock. He flashed me a relieved grin and said, "See you at eight, then."

The moment the door closed behind him, my brain fog evaporated. I dropped my head into my hands. What had I just agreed to do? Dating Nate was a bad idea. I was way too emotional about him. Leaving

Birch Springs would be that much harder if we got involved.

By the time I got home after work, I was a big knot of emotions again. I kept swinging between excitement and nervous anticipation and then regret and worry. Nate had actually asked me out! He'd picked me instead of those other girls from last night. But dating him was foolish, since I was planning on leaving soon.

Absolutely everything in my meager wardrobe was wrong. I hadn't thought to ask what he was planning for us to do. I didn't have many options as it was. What if he wanted to go hiking? Or to a fancy dinner? Or a concert? I tried on every possible combination of clothes before throwing up my hands in defeat.

"What's going on in here?" Mae asked tentatively from the doorway.

I froze and looked around. I was wearing two different shoes, and every article of clothing I owned was spread around the room.

"Nate asked me on a date for tonight, but I don't know where we're going or what we're doing, and I don't know what I should wear, and I think it was a mistake for me to go out with him, and I hate everything I own." I crumpled into a chair.

Mae, who was wearing an adorable work outfit, pressed her lips together, eyes sparkling. I couldn't resist a self-deprecating smile.

"So, you actually agreed to go on a date with Nate?"

She stepped into the room slowly, as if I was a dangerous animal who might attack at any moment.

"Yes," I admitted, rolling my eyes.

"He's pretty cute," she said slowly.

"Yes," I groaned.

"Okay, we can figure this out." Mae's voice became businesslike. "Where do you think he will take you?"

"I guess dinner?" I sat up a little. "I mean, he's always seemed like the kind of guy who wants to impress a girl. I would expect him to want to go somewhere that's expensive or trendy. But there isn't any place like that around here."

Mae tapped her chin thoughtfully. "There are a few restaurants within a forty-five minute drive."

"But that puts us arriving around nine. That's way too late for supper."

"That's true. Okay, I think your best option is a cute top with nice jeans and sandals. If you aren't going to a really fancy place, jeans would work for everything."

I slumped. "I don't have anything like that!"

"I bet Rosemarie does. She's taller than you, but you're about the same size everywhere else. Let's go ask her." Mae grabbed my hand and dragged me from the room. I clomped after her on uneven shoes.

Once Rosemarie was informed of the situation, she was quick to offer her entire wardrobe to me. Between the two girls, I was soon changing clothes in the second-floor bathroom that Jill and Rosemarie shared. We'd settled on a very nice pair of dark-blue jeans and a gray, sleeveless blouse that was flowy and shimmery. My feet were smaller than Rosemarie's, but she and Mae decided that my brown leather sandals would work with the ensemble.

By that point, they were invested in my date preparations, and we all trooped upstairs to make decisions about my hairstyle and makeup.

Their help was just what I needed. They had me laughing and forgetting all about my worries in no time. We had supper at the dining room table, and I felt a pleasant buzz of anticipation, nothing more. I refused to allow myself to think about the future. I liked Nate. He was attractive, fun, and actually sweet. I liked spending time with him. That was all I needed to think about. I would not worry about what was coming down the road. I would enjoy tonight and the fun of being with a guy I liked, who liked me back. End of story.

It was my night to help with cleanup, but Mae refused to let me risk splashing myself with dirty dishwater and insisted we swap chores. I swept the floor and was allowed to help clear the table, but then Jill and Rosemarie sat with me on the porch, keeping up a stream of light-hearted chatter.

The sun was getting low in the sky when Nate's Jeep appeared in the driveway.

"Have fun," Jill said and made a quick escape.

Rosemarie gave my arm a squeeze and flashed an excited grin, and she followed Jill back into the house.

I took a deep breath, grabbed my purse, and slowly made my way down the steps to meet Nate at his car.

"Hi," he said with a mostly-excited-but-slightly-nervous smile. "Are you ready?"

"You bet," I replied and climbed up into the seat beside him. "Where are we going?"

"Wait and see." Nate's smile turned mischievous.

The butterflies in my stomach gave an extra flutter.

11

I LIKE to think that I'm an open-minded, nonjudgmental type of person. I try really hard not to jump to conclusions or make assumptions about other people. But something about Nate had made me put on my super-springy judgment shoes, and I had jumped like I was an Olympian.

So I was completely and totally confused when he didn't get on the highway and drive to the nicest restaurant Melbourne had to offer. Instead, the Jeep turned off the two-lane county road and onto a dirt path. I would have bet everything I had that Nate would try and impress me with his money. Despite his apparent reform, I was sure that going on a date with him would result in a long evening of expensive and pretentious activities.

But that dirt road shattered all my expectations. What in the world was going on?

I was suddenly very glad that I was at least wearing jeans. Mae's advice was proving to be wise.

We only drove for a few minutes before the car slowed, and then came to a stop. Twilight was upon us, but Nate's flash of white teeth when he turned to me and smiled was still unmistakable.

"We're here," he announced.

I hoped the dark hid the skepticism that was sure to be apparent on my face. Reluctantly, I climbed down and then stood, feeling awkward while Nate rummaged around in the back of his Jeep. Finally, he emerged with a cardboard box in his arms.

"Follow me."

Since it was unlikely that he had a box full of weapons, I decided it wouldn't hurt to go along with him. I did lift up a quick prayer that I wouldn't be one of those girls who ended up on the news because she'd walked willingly into a dangerous situation when she knew she shouldn't, not wanting to be rude. I was so busy thinking that that sort of thing would totally happen to me that I didn't notice when Nate stopped.

"Here, have a seat," he said after placing the box on the ground.

I saw in the dim light that there were two camp chairs set up next to a makeshift fire pit. Oh, we were going to have a fire under the stars! My heart melted, and all thoughts of being murdered evaporated. This was so much better than a fancy supper somewhere. Was Nate only doing this because he knew I'd prefer it, or was this his idea of a romantic date, too? And did it matter if the former was true?

It took him less than a minute to coax sparks into flames. Then he settled back into the other camp chair next to me.

The flickering firelight lit up Nate's sea-green eyes, tanned skin, and white smile. I noticed that he'd shaved for this; his five o'clock shadow was gone. He was really too good-looking to be allowed. It wasn't fair.

"I hope you don't mind that I'm not taking you somewhere fancy. I took a risk. You're not the fancy sort of girl, so I thought that going somewhere quiet where we could just talk would be fun." His voice petered out.

I smiled and said, "I think it's a great idea. You're right, I'm not a fancy-restaurant type of girl."

He looked relieved and sat back, shoving his hands into his pockets, legs stretched out in front of him. "Okay, best restaurant you've ever eaten at?"

"That's way too hard! I could never pick the best, ever," I shot back.

"If you could pick one place you've eaten at to eat at again, no matter where it is in the world, where would you go?"

I mulled that over. "Probably this little hole-in-the-wall Thai place in Florida. Best Pad Thai I've ever eaten. What about you?"

We talked for a while as the stars blinked into the sky. Soon the dark expanse above us was punctuated with thousands of diamonds. Nate would get up periodically to toss a log onto the fire, and then sparks would spiral up, as though to join their cousins in the sky.

Our chairs were close enough that our arms brushed, and when it grew chilly, Nate put his arm around my shoulders. He had even brought marshmallows for roasting, and we enjoyed devouring the nutritionally-void treats. I was terrible at roasting them to the golden brown that I liked best. I always grew impatient and plunged them too close to the coals. Whenever I pulled out yet another fiery, blackening glob on the end of my stick, Nate would blow it out and then offer to swap for the perfectly toasted marshmallow on the end of his stick, insisting that he liked them burned.

The whole night was entirely magical. I was sorry when the last of the coals flickered out and we climbed into the Jeep and drove home. We rode in silence and I, for one, wanted to hold on to the happiness for as long as possible.

But too soon, Nate pulled to a stop in front of Bumblebee House and turned off the engine. We both stayed seated, casting shy glances at each other.

"I had a really good time," I said.

"So did I." Nate cleared his throat, his brow furrowing. "Listen, Emily, I wanted to make sure to say this before tonight ended, so that things wouldn't be weird."

I bit my lip. That didn't sound good.

He took a deep breath. "I want to be really clear about everything with you. I think I already told you that I like you a lot."

I nodded.

"Good. I want to date you because I want to get to know you romantically. This isn't a 'just friends' sort of thing for me." The light above the garage cast a warm glow over us, and Nate looked sweet and earnest.

I let out a breath I hadn't known I was holding and allowed a tiny smile to bloom. "Me either," I confessed.

"I joined a men's Bible study. Did I tell you that? I didn't? Well, it was after you... well, after you told me off." Nate looked away.

"I'm so sorry," I apologized again.

But he cut me off, eyes swinging fiercely to mine. "Don't be sorry, Em. I'm glad you said all of that. You were right about everything. I had gotten myself into a place where I didn't care about anyone but myself, and I was bored with me. I was such a jerk."

Not knowing what to say, I reached over and took his hand in mine. He squeezed it gently and smiled, eyes on our hands.

"Anyway, I joined this men's group because I knew that I needed to get everything back into focus, and the best place I know to make that happen is at church. So, I joined the group. Matt's in it, actually. Anyway, we've got a lot of single guys who are dating, and we're working really hard to do the right thing and set up healthy boundaries in our relationships."

I blinked in the dark, taken aback. This was not a conversation I ever expected to have, especially with Nate. Most guys were pawing at you the first chance they got. And here was Nate, setting up boundaries.

"I think that, for now, I'm not going to kiss you goodnight," he said quietly. "It's not because I don't want to, believe me. But we're just starting to date, and getting physical would skew our judgment. Don't you think?"

"Yeah," I stammered. "You're right."

"Okay. I'm going to walk you to the door and give you a goodnight hug, and it's not going to be weird."

We both laughed, since the entire conversation was precisely and exactly weird. But we did just as he said. We got out of the Jeep and Nate walked over to my side, took me by the hand, and we walked up to the front door.

"Goodnight, Emily. I had a wonderful time." He leaned forward and wrapped his arms around me.

I leaned into him, inhaling the aroma of woodsmoke and cologne. "I had a wonderful time, too."

And then he was heading back down the walk, waving over his shoulder and calling, "See you tomorrow at the Beanery!"

I floated inside.

MY SHIFT DIDN'T START until noon the next day, which was a good thing, since we didn't get home until after midnight. I slept late and finally went downstairs in search of breakfast around nine. Only Jill was still home, but she was quick to ask about my date.

"It was really good," I said dreamily. "He took me out where we could watch the stars and just sit around a fire and talk."

Jill didn't look convinced that this constituted a romantic date. She wasn't much of an outdoorsy girl and definitely would have preferred dinner at a restaurant to roasting marshmallows by a fire.

I giggled at her look of consternation. "Where did Marco take you on your first date?"

She glanced down at her sparkling engagement ring. "Gosh, it was so long ago I almost can't remember. Oh, no, I do remember! We went to the best sushi restaurant in Phoenix, and then to a Broadway show that was touring. I was so nervous, I kept dropping my chopsticks."

"Things turned out okay, though, right?"

"Of course they did. We're engaged." Jill's smile looked a little forced. "I mean, it's hard to be so far apart. But there aren't a lot of teaching jobs in my parents' town in Arizona, and Granddad was superintendent here. He sort of pulled strings to get me an interview."

"How did Marco feel about you moving so far away?" I'd never talked to Jill about her fiancé before, and I was glad for the opportunity. Of all the Bumblebee girls, she was the only one in a long-term relationship.

"At first, he didn't like it. But he's really focused on his career right now, so it ended up being a good thing. I wouldn't have seen him much anyway. He travels for work all the time."

Jill and Marco were engaged, even though they were several states apart. Would it be worth doing something like that with Nate if it came time for me to leave? Immediately, I pushed that thought away. I would not be the girl who analyzed her relationship to death. No. We were having fun now. Whatever happened would happen, and we would deal with it when it came.

"Do you have a wedding date picked out?" I asked, trying to keep the conversation light.

But Jill frowned and rolled her eyes. "Not yet. It's been two years and we haven't set a date. I keep trying to tell myself it doesn't matter. We'll get there when we get there, right?"

"Sure," I nodded supportively. However, I didn't leave the conversation feeling optimistic for them. It seemed as though Jill and Marco had some work to do on their relationship.

I went for a long run, letting music and my pounding heart keep me from dwelling on Nate. I took a shower and did a load of laundry. By the time I left for work, my damp hair in a long braid down my back,

I was ready for the day, ready to see Nate, and ready to let whatever was coming take its course.

"Hi," Sophie said around her snapping gum. "It's been totally quiet. Like, Walking Dead quiet. I'm going to take my break."

I watched her leave and suppressed a grin. I liked Sophie. Especially because her dramatic flair tended to make life interesting.

I busied myself with refilling cups and napkins, sweeping the café, and starting a fresh pot of decaf. Once everything was tidy, I allowed myself to peek at my phone. Nate had texted to ask if I was at work yet. I bit my lip, smiling like a fool, and replied that I was here.

Not ten minutes later, he pushed open the door and my heart leapt. Since no one else was there, I scooted around the corner and gave him a lingering hug.

"You always smell like coffee beans," he said with a grin.

Laughing, I said, "Well, I suppose I'll take that as a compliment."

"You should. All women should give up wearing perfume and just roll around in coffee beans."

I gave him a light punch on the arm before making my way back to the register and taking his order. As I busied myself with grinding beans and making foamy milk, Nate told me about his day.

"Dad wants me to take the lead on a new project. He says he likes my work lately and thinks I should start taking on more responsibility around the company."

"That's great! What's the project?"

Nate explained about a building that was scheduled to go up and how his father's firm would be involved. As I handed over his steaming cup, he said, "Anyway, we should go out to celebrate."

Fireworks went off in my stomach, and I beamed at him. "Okay!"

1 2

———————

OVER THE NEXT WEEK, I couldn't stop smiling. Nate dropped by the Beanery every day. We saw each other at the ranch, and I loved watching his gentle care of the kids. He took me on a date, and this time we did go to Melbourne. We ate at a funky diner and then sat together, holding hands and watching a movie.

But no matter how happy I was when we were together, there was a voice whispering in my ear whenever I was alone, saying it wouldn't last. Sometimes, when I thought about a future that meant staying here in Birch Springs with Nate, I felt panicky. I was not made to stay in one place. As much as I liked Birch Springs and loved the Bumblebee girls, I hated the idea of being chained here with no escape option. I needed to always have option A (staying in one place) and option B (leaving whenever I wanted) and secret option C (being able to pack my car and be gone in under an hour).

The only way I could find to cope was to thoroughly push away all thoughts of the future. I refused to have conversations with Nate about anything beyond the next week. It seemed to bother him, but things were still too new between us for him to actually broach the topic.

He came dancing into the Beanery one Wednesday morning and leaned across the counter to give me a hug. "Can you take a quick break? I want to talk to you about something."

I glanced over at Sophie, who popped her gum and gave me the thumbs-up. Nate wasted no time in grabbing my hand the moment I rounded the counter and dragging me to the sidewalk outside.

"What's up?" I tried to reassure my pounding heart that nothing was wrong, but it seemed determined to race no matter what I told it.

Nate broke out in a grin. "They're selling tickets for the annual gala event, and I wanted to know if I should buy tickets for us."

I took a deep breath. Oh, so that was it. No big deal. "When is the gala?"

"September," he said, and then made a please-don't-get-mad grimace.

I blinked rapidly, my fingers growing numb and my stomach instantly beginning to churn. September? It didn't seem to matter that I'd planned to stay in Birch

Springs for a full year, which meant until the following June. It didn't matter that I would probably really enjoy going to the gala with Nate. All I could think about was committing to something so far in advance. It put pressure on us to remain a couple, and I just didn't know what was going to happen.

Fingers fiddling with my belt, I bit my lip and shrugged. "I don't know."

Nate put a hand on my elbow and leaned over. He was all gentle concern as he asked, "Why don't you want to go?"

How could I tell him the truth? How could I say that I wasn't sure we'd still be dating in September? It was so fatalistic, yet it was all I could think about. I shrugged lamely.

"Is it the formal dress part? I know you aren't all about dressing up, but we could go shopping together, and I could help you find something that would be great. My dad's been dragging me there for years, so I know exactly what you should wear."

"That's nice of you," I said with a weak smile.

His face took on a look of confident condescension that jerked my panic into annoyance. "I know you don't like to plan ahead. I get it, Em, I really do. But I have to buy these tickets now. Sometimes, you do have to plan ahead."

I pulled my elbow from his hand and scowled at him. "Stop talking to me like I'm five, Nate. I don't appreciate it."

He threw up his hands. "I'm trying to be understanding and give you space, but I don't have any more time to wait on buying tickets."

"I don't care if you buy tickets or not. Buy them, and when September comes, we'll see whether or not I'm still the girl you want to take to the gala." My eyes felt hot, and I knew I was about to burst into over-dramatic tears.

Real understanding washed over Nate, and the obnoxious version of himself disappeared. He stepped closer and shoved his hands into his pockets, since I was still bristling.

As gently as he could, he assured me, "I'm going to want to take you to the gala in September, Emily. That isn't going to change."

His kindness was the key that my emotions apparently needed, and tears began to trickle down my cheeks. I wiped at them, embarrassed.

Nate pulled me into a careful hug and held me as he rubbed my back. I laid my head on his shoulder and let the fear and worry slip away along with my tears. When I finally pulled away, the worst of them were gone, though their roots were still tangled deep inside me.

"Is that what this is about?" Nate asked quietly. "Are you afraid that we aren't going to be together for long?"

"It's stupid," I replied. I kicked at the sidewalk, refusing to meet his eyes.

"It's not stupid. Fear of commitment is super-common."

"Thanks, Oprah," I retorted.

Nate's hands went to his hips, and I knew I'd struck a nerve. I didn't want him mad at me, but I didn't want him lecturing me either.

"What do you want me to say? You seem determined to push me away no matter what."

I glanced at him then and saw the irritation on his face. It felt terrible to know that this guy, who I really, really liked, was frustrated with me. I had no idea what the future held, and I didn't want to make Nate promises I couldn't keep, but I didn't want to stop dating him. That would be awful.

Sighing, I apologized. "I'm sorry. This is a hard topic for me. I think I need time and space to figure out what my next steps are supposed to be."

Nate rubbed the back of his neck. "Okay. Does that mean you want me to leave you alone?"

"No," I almost shouted.

His sea-green eyes met mine and they were so full that I bit my lip. It was such a relief to see that he didn't want that either. Nate was trying to do the right thing where I was concerned. That calmed my panic enough for me to move forward.

"I want to keep dating you. I like seeing you every day. I just don't know what is going to happen a month from now. When you talk about plans for the future, all

I hear is that I have to promise to stay here. I'm not ready to make that promise."

My words found fertile ground. He nodded gravely. "I guess I'll buy tickets to the gala and hope you're still around."

"Okay," I whispered.

He turned and walked away without another word. I felt awful.

When I arrived home after work, I changed into my oldest PJs and went in search of something comforting to drink. I was just adding the teabag to my cup of boiling water when Rosa walked in.

"Uh-oh. Herbal tea in the middle of the afternoon? Are you sick, or having man trouble?" Her brown eyes sparkled playfully.

I offered a sorry attempt at a smile and continued dunking the bag up and down.

"Could you use some company?" Rosa offered.

"Sure."

Soon the older woman had her cup ready and led the way out to the veranda, as she called it, where we sat under a pergola with climbing roses. Bees were busily working around us, adding their hum to the quiet background music of summer. It was lovely and I tried to appreciate it, but I was largely unsuccessful. My brain was full of Nate and the pain I'd caused him.

"How are things going with Nate?" inquired Rosa, somehow knowing exactly what was on my mind.

I pulled my legs up onto the chair and rested my

forehead on my knees for a moment, cup forgotten on the table next to me. Rosa didn't seem to mind that I took a full minute before answering. I couldn't seem to find words. My emotions and fears swirled around, choking out any clear thoughts I might have had.

"I think there's something wrong with me," I finally spluttered.

She raised an arched eyebrow and sipped at her tea with her firecracker-red lips.

I gulped air and dove in. "I like Nate. A lot. More than anyone I've ever liked before. But when I think of settling down here, I panic. All I can think about is, 'Get away, Emily!' He asked me to go with him to some gala at his work in September. September! That's only two months away, but I flipped out."

"What are you afraid of?" Rosa asked calmly.

"What if we're not together in September? He'll have bought those tickets for nothing." I looked at Rosa as the words hovered around us. She gave me a little smile, and I thought about what I'd said. So what if we weren't dating? Nate could find a date. Unused tickets weren't a big deal. I allowed myself a little chuckle at the silliness of that fear.

Rosa adjusted her blue cotton skirt. "What are you afraid of?" she repeated.

I bit my lip and considered. "I'm not sure," I whispered.

"That's fair."

I rolled my eyes. "It's lame. Why don't I know what

I'm scared of?"

"I think it's easier to run away than to face our fears, don't you? When you've experienced the loss of someone you love, it's that much more difficult to go back and try again. Believe me, I know." Rosa sighed.

"How did you know I've lost someone?" I asked, finally sipping my tea.

The perfectly coiffed brunette shrugged. "An educated guess, I suppose. Did I guess right?"

"You did. I lost my mom and brother when I was eight. It was just me and my dad after that, and things were never the same. Dad was lost in his grief and didn't know what to do with his daughter. We never seemed to know what to say to each other anymore." I was surprised to find myself opening up to Rosa. There was something about her calm demeanor that made it easy to give voice to things I usually kept quiet.

"I think that makes a lot of sense, then," she said thoughtfully. "You've been hurt and gotten out of the habit of being close to people."

I rolled that idea around in my brain. It did make sense. "How do I figure out how to be normal?"

Rosa laughed. "You're asking the wrong person! I gave up on normalcy a long time ago. But, as to how to let people in, I think you're just going to have to practice. Open up to a few folks that you know are likely to be trustworthy."

Just listening to her talk about it made my palms sweaty and my stomach turn over.

Either my panic was written plainly across my face, or else Rosa was a psychic. She patted my hand, and I swung wide eyes to her.

"Relationships are messy, Emily. That's okay. We're all sinful, selfish people trying to interact. It takes grace and forgiveness to exist in good relationships of any kind. We'll always step on each other's toes and have our feelings hurt. That's not a reason to avoid all relationships. The price we pay for little hurts is pennies compared to the millions that you receive in return. Take the risk. I promise, you'll regret it if you don't."

In Rosa's voice, I heard a lifetime of experience in investing in relationships and fully knowing regret for opportunities she didn't take. I wasn't sure how old she was. Late 30s? Early 40s? Not so far from my twenty-six years, but I had a feeling that Rosa had loved deeply and was richer for it, though there was a twang of regret in her voice that sparked my curiosity.

She gave my hand a final pat and, with a brief excuse of some undone chore, she left me alone with my thoughts. I watched her swish away in her cool, vintage outfit. Rosa was running this house and keeping an eye on all of us younger women. I'd seen her interact with the people of the community. She knew them, and they knew her.

I wasn't sure if I was brave enough to tie myself to one place like she had. How did you choose where to invest yourself? And what if I chose wrong?

13

I SPENT the rest of the day doing little things to make my world feel better. I vacuumed my room, cleaned the bathroom Mae and I shared, and went to the grocery store to restock my stash of snacks. Jill came home and asked if I wanted to watch a movie with her. It turned out that we both liked old Doris Day films and we settled on "Calamity Jane," which was delightful.

It was my turn to help with supper. Rosemarie was home, and the two of us put together a chicken taco bar fit for a king. The other girls were only too glad to heap their taco shells with all the fixings we'd prepared.

My phone rang as Rosa and Mae took over cleanup, and I headed toward the stairs when I saw it was Nate calling. I wanted some privacy for this conversation.

"Hi," I said as I took the stairs two at a time.

"Hi," Nate said back.

A little shiver went up my spine at the sound of his voice. I could picture his beautiful green eyes and hoped they were crinkling up in a smile, which was how I liked them best. Or had I caused too much drama today to make him smile now?

"I'm glad you called. I feel awful about earlier, and I don't like leaving things in a weird place."

"Hey, it's really okay. It wasn't a fun conversation, but I think it was one we needed to have."

I reached my room and went straight to the little chair next to the window overlooking the back yard, thankful that I no longer kept my phone in my car. I curled up and agreed, "You're probably right. I talked with Rosa when I came home, and she sort of challenged me on some things."

"How are you feeling now?"

"Good, I think." I laughed a little. "I mean, I still have a lot to mull over."

"Well, I'm here if you ever want to talk." He paused before charging on. "Listen, Em, I know the timing of this is pretty awful, but there's not a lot I can do about it."

"Oh no," I moaned. "What?"

"I told my parents that I was dating someone, and my mother insisted that I invite you over for Sunday lunch. Now, before you freak out, just know that this doesn't mean we're more serious than we actually are. Meeting my family isn't some way for me to trap you."

He sighed. "If I could put it off, I would, but my mom really wants to meet you."

I fought the panic that was rising. Nate didn't think this meant too much. It wasn't his idea. I tried to remember what Rosa had said about investing in relationships. I liked meeting new people. I could meet Nate's parents and still move away when the time came, couldn't I?

And that's how I found myself wearing my best dress and sandals, nervously holding Nate's hand as he led the way up the walk to a pristine and very large house that Sunday.

He stopped at the door and turned to me with a worried expression. "Thanks for doing this."

Nate had been quiet ever since he'd picked me up. It was only making my nerves worse. What was he afraid of? I tried not to let his worry crank my anxiety up any higher.

So, I squeezed his hand and said, "If it helps you out, I'm glad to do it."

He gave me a brave smile before turning the knob and leading the way into the house. I followed him and felt like I'd stepped into something out of a magazine. Everything was gleaming, on trend, and spotless. Bumblebee House could have been featured in a magazine, but it was warm and inviting with interesting artwork and fun nooks and crannies. The Weisert home was more like a museum where they scolded you for touching things. I half expected there to be velvet ropes keeping guests away from the valuable knickknacks.

Nate's mother came bustling into the hallway.

"Nate!" she cried and opened her arms to give him a very stiff hug.

"Hi, Mom. This is Emily. Emily, this is my mother, Gail." Nate stepped back from his mother's arms and gestured to me.

"It's nice to meet you, Emily," Gail said. She held out a manicured hand and gave my fingers a single squeeze. "Let's go out to the deck. Your father is grilling steaks. Would you like something to drink?"

Gail clacked off toward the back of the house, her beige palazzo pants swinging and her fitted beige top completing her monochromatic look. She was petite but wearing heels inside the house to compensate. I had the impression that shoes were a part of the outfit, and therefore a mandatory part of the appearance of the house's occupants.

Once we were given sparkling water in glass bottles, we were instructed to follow Gail to the deck, where I was introduced to Bruce, Nate's dad. Bruce was balding and loud, but a good deal warmer than his wife. We only had a few minutes of awkwardness before the sound of a car pulling up reached our ears.

"That must be Lucy," Gail announced as she sprang to her feet.

"My sister," Nate whispered as his mother disappeared into the house.

"So, Emily, what is it you do?" Bruce asked.

"At the moment, I'm a barista at the Birch Springs Beanery." It felt small to admit it here in this big, fancy house. "My degree's in biology, though."

Bruce waved his grilling flipper at Nate. "Your generation is all about earning degrees they never use. Nate has a degree in marketing, but he hasn't put it to much use."

For some reason, Bruce's words seemed to carry more weight than his friendly smile would admit. Beside me, Nate shifted uncomfortably.

"I've used my degree before. I was working for a conservation group out in Oregon before coming here." I tried not to sound defensive.

"Well, that's something, at least. I suppose there aren't too many jobs for a biology major here in Birch Springs," Bruce chuckled brassily.

The French doors opened, and Gail returned with a younger version of herself, Nate's sister Lucy. I shook Lucy's hand before her father asked about the latest case she was working on. Nate had explained earlier that his sister was the youngest lawyer to make partner in the history of her firm. So, I wasn't surprised when Lucy launched into a complicated legal explanation, which I didn't even pretend to follow. By the time she finished, we were sitting around the shaded patio table with our plates full.

I had to admit that the food looked great. Gail had confessed to buying everything already made at a gourmet shop in Melbourne. Since I couldn't picture her actually risking her manicure or doing anything practical, that made a lot of sense, and I dug in eagerly.

As the meal progressed, I found myself watching Nate more and more. His family was never rude to me, but I was certainly an afterthought. They'd dismissed me almost as soon as they'd met me, which suited me fine. I wouldn't have had any idea how to contribute to their lengthy discussion of whether or not Aunt Martha had had a tummy tuck. What was intriguing was the way they kept trying to push Nate back into the role of high school football star.

"How's work going?" Lucy asked him at one point. "Dad said you were going to be in charge of a project." The way she said it made me think of an adult bending over, hands on knees, talking down to a child.

"He's leading one now," Bruce answered before Nate could open his mouth. "He's really leading the way. The guys on his team weren't too happy when I picked him to take lead, but they're coming around. I guess it pays to be the boss's son after all."

Nate smiled uncomfortably, refusing to meet my eyes.

"Don't you think it's time that we replaced your car, Nate?" Gail changed the subject brightly. "That Jeep of yours is awful. We could get you something new. Bruce, you could work out a deal with Carl over at the dealership, couldn't you?"

"Mom, I don't want a new car. I like the one I have.

Besides, I'm an adult now and if I want a new car, I'll buy one myself." I could tell Nate was trying not to sound petulant.

Gail waved his words away with a swish of her hand. "We're glad to do it. You're working hard, and your father and I appreciate it, don't we, Bruce?"

"You bet," Bruce agreed with too much gusto. "We got Lucy her Audi when she made partner. It's what parents do for their kids."

I looked down at my plate and bit my lip to keep from smiling. If Bruce knew that I drove a beat-up old minivan, he'd probably keel over. Or threaten me with a new car.

"Did you get your tickets for the gala?" Lucy steered the conversation in a new direction.

Nate's eyes checked to make sure I was okay with this topic before he said, "I did."

"Are you taking Emily?" Gail pried. Then she laughed carelessly. "If you haven't asked her yet, I might have just put my foot in my mouth."

"Oh, you have to come," Lucy cooed and patted at my arm with her long fingernails. "It's always so much fun. I've been shopping for my dress for a month. I think I finally found something in Denver that will work. What do you think about flying down for the weekend sometime so we could buy it, Mom?"

The two women discussed their plans and effectively shut the rest of us out. I watched Nate, who was staring down at his food with determination. My heart squeezed for him. I would have bet everything I had that before I'd yelled at him all those weeks ago, Nate would have found this sort of conversation normal. He might even have jumped in and swam around. But now he saw it as shallow and empty and, from the look on his face, he was uncomfortable with that realization.

Bruce vacillated between praising his son for his work at the firm and chastising him for not branching out on his own. Every compliment was laced with a hint that Nate was riding his father's coattails.

"Nate here really impressed the board at our last meeting. That'll come in handy when you take over after I retire. Heh, heh, at least I don't have to worry about handing my company over to someone else, since you seem intent on sticking around!"

Gail moved on to discussing the redecorating plans of everyone she knew. Lucy regaled the table with stories of her high school friends who had botched plastic surgeries, unfortunate children, or failed marriages.

When we were finally able to leave, we got into the car silently. Nate put on his reflective sunglasses, clenched his jaw, and drove away as though he was eager to put as much space as possible between himself and his family. We weren't more than a mile down the road, though, when he suddenly signaled and turned off onto a dirt road.

I had a feeling that we were headed somewhere he

knew well. And, sure enough, Nate drove expertly up the winding hills until he pulled to a stop at a rocky outcropping. He got out of the car and slammed the door, then came around to my side and held my door open for me. I climbed down, and Nate took my hand in his.

We walked to a large, flat rock that overlooked Birch Springs and the surrounding country. Nate sat with his back against a rock and pulled me down to sit with him. I settled between his legs and leaned back against his chest. I laid my head back so that my forehead rested against his cheek and threaded my fingers through his.

We sat like that for a long time. No words were necessary. I don't know if Nate could have expressed what he was feeling in that moment. It was just too big. Before long, it grew hot out there and we couldn't stay any longer.

Wordlessly, we got back into the Jeep and rode back to town. But now, Nate held my hand as we drove, rubbing his thumb over mine. The stings he'd gathered during lunch had been plucked out while we sat on the rock. I was glad to have been there for him, even though I hadn't said anything.

When he pulled up at Bumblebee House, I turned to him and waited.

Finally, he put his head back on the head rest and looked over at me. "Thanks for coming with me today. I didn't realize how much I would need you."

I smiled gently and reached out my hand to run the backs of my fingers over his cheek. He grabbed my hand and pressed it to his lips.

"Of course." Then I climbed down from the Jeep and headed into the house.

14

<hr>

It felt like Nate and I had reached a new level in our relationship. We'd walked a little deeper into the pool together, hand in hand. It was both exciting and scary, to be honest. But as the next week slipped by, we both relished this new place. Our arrival had been hard-won.

Unfortunately, Nate was spending more and more time at the Beanery when he should have been at work. His midmorning coffee breaks were drawing out to a half-hour, then forty-five minutes, then an hour. I was at a loss as to what I should do. I'd had no trouble confronting him about my perceptions of his deficits before we were dating. Now that I had a better understanding of his family's situation, I was reluctant to say anything.

I mean, I'd met his father. I knew now that working with Bruce had to be difficult for Nate. I totally got it.

But I found myself biting my tongue and forcing myself to find some distraction rather than obsessing over how long he sat in the café, sipping his coffee and playing on his phone.

I was also afraid, all of a sudden, of having another confrontation. We were in such a nice place. The rosy glow of sitting on the rock together was filling all of our interactions with a lovely sweetness. I feared that bringing up my concerns would shatter the glow.

So I didn't say anything. I told myself firmly that it was Nate's business, not mine.

Nate liked surprising me with fun activities for our dates. He put a lot of thought into finding things we could do together that we would both enjoy. For the most part, I really enjoyed this. It was so sweet that he wanted to share his favorite local haunts, and that he paid attention to what I might like.

When he loaded me into his Jeep and started the drive to Melbourne on my next day off, I sat back and looked forward to the day ahead. I was sporting a pair of cutoff khakis and a "Pure Michigan" t-shirt, as well as my Idaho trucker's hat. It wasn't a glamorous outfit, but Nate never commented on what I wore. After meeting his mother, who was sure to have drilled him in the importance of appearance all his life, I appreciated this even more.

He turned into the parking lot for a mall and my curiosity was piqued. Was there an old merry-go-round here that he'd ridden as a kid? Maybe he'd found a store that specialized in Wyoming paraphernalia.

I took his hand, and we walked together toward an entrance for one of the department stores. Nate was busy telling me a long story about when he'd come to Melbourne in high school to play football, and the whole team had gotten food poisoning at a local diner.

My brain was whirling, trying to find clues as to why we were here. Surely it wasn't to eat at that diner. That would be one Nate Weisert landmark I would be all too happy to avoid.

Nate led me inside and around to the women's section. Then he turned to me with an anticipatory grin. "Today, we're going shopping!"

I gave the racks a raised eyebrow and said, "Are you taking up cross-dressing?"

He laughed merrily. "No, silly. We're shopping for you!"

I paused and let that sink in. Okay. Shopping. "For the gala?"

"We can."

So, buying a gala dress was not the goal. The rosy glow was definitely retreating hastily. I tried to keep my annoyance to a manageable level.

"What is it exactly that you think I need to buy?" I crossed my arms and took a steadying breath.

"Don't get mad," Nate wheedled. "It's not that I don't think you look good, because you definitely do. But you have, like, one dress and one pair of jeans and two pairs of shoes. If we're going to be going out, you'll probably want to have something else to wear, right?"

I blew out my breath and clenched my toes to keep my anger from taking over. "That might be true, but I don't want more clothes. If I need something, Rosemarie lets me borrow it."

"Come on, all women love shopping." He grabbed my hand and gave it a teasing squeeze.

I pulled it out of his grip. Nate clearly didn't understand how close I was to blowing my top. How could we have been dating this long, and he didn't get this about me? Or did he hope I would somehow be different, more like the kind of girls he usually dated? The thought made my stomach clench.

"I don't love shopping. I don't want to have a huge wardrobe. I like being able to fit everything I own in my van. I like being able to pack up and leave town in under an hour. If I wanted more clothes, Nate, I would buy them for myself." My voice was low and firm and quivering with frustration.

His face clouded over. He glanced around to make sure the salesladies were out of earshot. "I thought that maybe, since things were going well with us, that you might be thinking about staying in Birch Springs. Are you seriously telling me that you still need to be able to leave at a moment's notice?"

I squirmed. That was a question I'd been avoiding. "I don't know."

I chanced a glance at him and saw that I'd hurt his

feelings. It made me mad. Why did Nate get to be the victim here?

"Why do you want me to have more clothes? Am I embarrassing you or something?" I shot back, taking the offensive.

"I already told you that I think you look good. I thought this would be fun. I guess I was wrong." He put his hands up in surrender. "I figured that things were going well for us and that you might be changing your mind about leaving so soon. I mean, you ripped a hole in your jeans when we were at the ranch last week. I thought you might need a new pair."

It was a fair point. I was now down to one pair of jeans, and I'd had them since college. It would be nice to have a few outfits that were just right for going out with Nate. But my pride was not going to let me surrender so easily.

But then he added, "Besides, if you're going to see my family again, you're going to need a new dress. Since we're here, let's just buy one."

His words were a punch right into that already-bruised part of my heart. He was embarrassed by how I dressed. Had his mother said something to him? Had she pointed out how obviously poorly matched we were? I thought back to the girls at the Talent Show who wore cute summer dresses that were fashionable and flattering. They'd been perfectly made up and walked confidently in high-heeled sandals.

I was never going to be one of those girls. Usually

that thought didn't bother me one iota. Now, though, I felt small and insufficient, and it made me even angrier than I already was.

He'd threaded his way through the racks and begun to flip through the clothes. He turned and held one up as if it was a peace offering. "What do you think of this one?"

The dress was gorgeous. The blue tones would complement my pale skin and black hair perfectly. Part of me itched to try it on and watch Nate's reaction when I floated out of the dressing room in it.

But most of me felt humiliated and angry, and I just wanted to get away. Without answering, I turned and walked down the aisle and into the mall. I gulped deep breaths until I found a women's restroom and flung myself inside. I dove into the first open stall and managed to lock the door before I burst into tears.

Once the wave of emotion receded, I took stock of myself. I was leaning against the door in a public bathroom stall, crying because my boyfriend had taken me shopping.

"Oh, Emily, get it together," I whispered raggedly. "You are officially a mess."

Shame was quickly filling the spaces where fear and embarrassment had been only moments before. I was making a stupendous fool of myself. Why was this so overwhelming?

"Emily?" Nate's voice called into the bathroom.

"You can't come in, this is a women's bathroom," I yelled back, pointing out the obvious.

"You're the only one in here," he answered after a moment's thought. "Right?"

When no other female voices hollered at him to leave, Nate's footsteps sounded across the tile floor. "Tell me you're not actually in here using the toilet. That would officially make this the most awkward thing I've ever done on a date."

I let loose a snotty, gurgling laugh. "No."

"Thank goodness for that." He was right outside the door. There was another pause, and then he sighed. "I think I've been an idiot."

"Well, that makes two of us," I said and pressed my forehead against the door. Somehow, it was easier to talk to him with the closed stall door between us.

"Can you tell me what's wrong? And this time I'll actually listen."

"I don't know if I have the right words. Plus, it might take a while."

There were the unmistakable sounds of Nate taking a seat on the floor outside the stall. "Go for it. Things might get weird if another woman comes in, but there aren't a lot of people at the mall on a Wednesday morning, so we might be okay."

The silence stretched, and I lifted up a desperate plea to find some way to explain to Nate, and probably to myself, what was going on in my head.

"What did I do wrong?" he asked again. Nate's voice was quiet and serious and hurt.

"You meant well," I began slowly. I had to repair the damage I'd caused before explaining the damage he'd caused. "I want to believe that you just wanted to do something you thought I'd enjoy."

"That's true."

"But when you mentioned your mom, I started feeling so inadequate."

"Why?" Nate sounded genuinely surprised.

I rolled my eyes. This was just like a guy. "Your parents' house is really nice, and your mom is perfectly put together. So's your sister. I was afraid that you wanted me to be more like them and less like me."

"Oh," he said. "That would be an awful feeling."

"Yeah." I took a shaky breath. It was time to be the brave woman I always thought I was. "Nate, I freak out whenever you talk about me sticking around. I know you know that, but I don't think I've told you why.

"My mom and my brother were killed in a car accident when I was eight. After that, Dad was so upset about losing Mom and David that he became like a robot. He would go to work, come home, bring something for supper, and then sit and watch TV. He hardly talked to me.

"Even though I was eight, I knew it was because he was so very, very sad. I started putting myself to bed and making my own lunches and doing my own laundry. I had to care for myself. We moved every couple of years, because Dad was in the Army. I always wanted to have friends, but going over to their houses was too hard. It made me see what was missing from mine."

I pressed my lips together as the hurt from my childhood pressed me from all sides, robbing me of breath momentarily. When it relented a little, I went on. "I don't understand why I'm so scared to be stuck in one place. I really like you, and I like hanging out together. There's nowhere else I want to be, but the thought of not being able to go if I need to terrifies me."

I bit my lip and waited for Nate to say something.

Finally, he said, "I'm terrified that I'll wake up one day and you'll be gone without another word. That's what scares me, Emily. Every time you talk about needing to leave, I just hear you saying that you might need to leave me."

I let those words sink in. I hadn't thought about it from his perspective.

"This is probably the most unromantic place to say this, but I'm in love with you," Nate said fervently. "I want to have a future that includes you in it."

My head tipped up and I blinked at the ceiling. How did I feel about that? Was I glad? Partly. Was I scared? Partly, too. I reached down and unlocked the bathroom door. When it swung out of the way, I saw Nate sitting on the floor, leaning against the wall, waiting for me to say something to his declaration of love. A crazy part of my brain wondered if seeing me in all my blotchy, snotty glory would cause him to retract his words.

I stepped over and slid down onto the floor next to him. I slipped my arm through his and put my head on his shoulder. He turned his head and kissed my forehead. Why were things so much clearer to me when we were sitting together, not talking? If only we could stay like this forever, everything would be fine.

"What do you want to do now?" he asked after a few minutes. I couldn't tell if he was disappointed that I hadn't told him I loved him back.

"I do need a new pair of jeans," I said.

"Are you sure?" He turned those beautiful eyes to me. "We don't have to."

I nodded. "I know. Since we're here, though, we should probably get a pair."

Nate pushed himself to his feet, then reached down a hand and pulled me up. When I was standing, he didn't immediately let go of my hand. Only inches spanned the gap between us, but there was too much in that space. I knew that if I'd told him I loved him, he would be kissing me. The fact that he wasn't was far more painful than I would have imagined. And I had no one to blame but myself.

15

IT HELPED to move back to the department store and busy ourselves examining their selection of jeans. Nate had far better taste in clothes than I did, and he soon had me heading back to the dressing room with a stack to try on. Each time I emerged from the dressing room, he had thoughtful comments that helped me to select the right pair.

We were walking to the front to pay when we passed that beautiful blue dress.

"Hang on," I said. I reached for one in my size. "Do you mind if I try this on?"

Nate answered carefully. "I don't mind, but you don't have to."

"I know," I smiled.

The attendant unlocked the dressing room for me with a sigh, as though I'd pulled her from some massively important task. Since she'd been folding shirts with all the speed of a sloth, I could only roll my eyes unsympathetically as the door closed behind me.

I pulled the dress over my head and looked at myself in the mirror. I loved it. It was a simple thing without sleeves or buttons or belt. In fact, it was exactly my style. It was pretty and not a bit fussy. I looked myself over critically. I liked it, but what would Nate think?

Feeling more apprehensive than before, I unlocked the door and walked out. He was sitting in a chair, flipping through his phone. When he sensed I was near, he looked up with an expectant smile which froze as he registered my appearance.

For two heartbeats, I had no idea what he was thinking. Was I wrong? Was it awful?

"Wow," he said breathlessly. "Wow, you look beautiful."

I felt my cheeks grow warm. "I really like this dress."

Nate's eyes were glued to my face. "Beautiful," he repeated.

I almost couldn't breathe myself. He wasn't talking about the dress. He was talking about me. "I, um, think I'll get it, then," I mumbled and hurried back to the dressing room.

As I pulled on my shorts and t-shirt, I caught sight of my flustered face in the mirror. Holy cow. Nate was in love with me. He thought I was beautiful. He wanted to have me around for a long time. All of it clicked together like it hadn't before, and I felt myself immersed in what he'd said to me. Nate was all-in.

Was I?

I paid for the dress and jeans, and then Nate suggested a good spot to get lunch. Within a half-hour we were sitting at a table by the window, eating hamburgers.

"So, why aren't you at work today?" I finally asked. If he was in love with me, I figured he would be willing to put up with me being direct again. My pep talk to myself in the bathroom stall had given me new courage. "You've been hanging around the café a lot more, too. I thought you were leading a project."

He looked up, eyes widely innocent, and shrugged. "They don't really need me."

I raised my eyebrows skeptically.

"Dad only put me in charge because I'm his son. I don't have the seniority for anyone to take me seriously. The project will be fine without me." He looked away, rueful.

I chewed for a minute. Poor Nate. "You got a degree in marketing, right? What job would you rather be doing?"

Another shrug. "It's funny. All the time growing up, people would ask me what I wanted to be when I grew up. I always said I wanted to be a football player or a businessman like my dad. Everyone seemed okay with those answers. But I never really knew what I wanted to do with my life. Everything that sounds interesting is impossible." He was instantly downhearted. This was clearly a fight he'd lost with himself long ago.

"Okay, what sounds interesting, then?" I pressed.

He smiled sadly. "I think it would be cool to be a nature photographer."

I nodded and waited. When he ducked his head without going on, I asked, "Why is that impossible?"

"It's hard to break into that industry. Everyone wants to be a photographer these days. There's no chance that I'd ever make a living doing it."

He wasn't wrong. But I hated the way he was so adamant about not even trying. "Do you own a camera? Have you taken photos you like?"

"Yeah. I've done a few, but they aren't anything special."

"Did you enjoy the process of taking them?"

He nodded. "I did. It felt really restful and fun. I showed them to my mom once, and she was polite but wasn't impressed. She told me I'd be better off focusing on my career."

I dipped a fry in ketchup and tried to pick my next words carefully. "Can I tell you what I think?"

"Of course."

"You might not like it."

"Well, since we're getting pretty good at difficult conversations, I say, bring it on." He winked at me, attempting to lighten the mood.

I smiled back. "Okay, then. I think that you should take nature photos if you love it. Clearly, it's a restful thing for you that refreshes you and gets you excited about life. Maybe with practice you'll be good enough to sell some. Maybe not. Even if you can't make a living at it, you should still do it."

He sighed. "I know." He trailed a fry through his blob of ketchup for a moment before cutting to the heart of the matter. "It's just hard to have to go to work some place that I don't care about at all."

"Sure, but that's just for now. If you do your best here at this job, another opportunity will open up down the road. If you've been a project manager for your dad, that will look amazing on your resume. The hard work you put in now will pay off."

Nate played with his napkin. "I hate that my dad thinks he has to hand me these jobs. It's like he believes I'll never make anything of myself."

I took his hand in mine. "He's wrong." Nate's eyes finally met mine. "He doesn't know what you can do. If you give this job your all, he'll see how incredible you are. And if he doesn't, you'll have worked hard, given it your best, and learned all you can. Then you can go on to whatever comes next as a better man."

I want to believe that a fire was lit in Nate, but that might have been too much to hope for. He smiled at me and thanked me, and the afternoon went on well. With all my heart, I wanted Nate to reach his true potential. Unfortunately, I was fighting against a lifetime of his family's weird lack of expectations for him. He himself had been fully believing those lies up until only a few weeks ago.

We poked around an old record store after lunch and took a walk along the river in the park. Nate dropped me off at home in midafternoon. It felt like we were back on solid ground after our shaky trip to the mall.

I scampered upstairs, hung my new dress in my closet, and put my new jeans in the drawer next to my other pair. I tried to fill my afternoon with things that would take my mind off the weirdness of that morning, but my brain kept revisiting the conversation we had.

I'd escaped to the front porch with a glass of iced tea and a mystery novel, which I wasn't reading, when Mae arrived home from work earlier than usual.

"My boss is leading a conference that all the senior people are attending, so he closed the office early and sent the rest of us home," she explained and settled into a cushioned chair next to me. "How was your date with Nate?"

I gave her a brief recap of the day and leaned my head back against the chair when I finished. "Why am I so clear and focused on what other people need and a total mess when it comes to my own stuff?"

"Because you're human," Mae answered wryly. We exchanged a smile before she went on, "Seriously, though, we all have that problem. I think it's because we have way too much background information about ourselves. I mean, you see some girl in a bad relationship with an abusive guy, and it's obvious she should leave him. But, for the girl, it isn't that simple. She sees all the good times they had, her fear of being alone, the complications of leaving him, and all that. It clouds her judgment."

"Ugh. I totally get that."

I could feel Mae looking at my profile thoughtfully. "So, Emily, what's the background stuff that's influencing this particular problem?"

Normally, I would have dodged the question. This time, though, I looked over at her and found that I wanted to talk it over with her. Maybe then I'd find some answers. I explained about losing my mom and my brother and how hard things were with my dad.

She listened, head tilted and looking like a little red bird. "Why does that make it so hard for you to stay in one place? Why are you so afraid of being connected to other people?"

"Because the people you love can be ripped away," I said without even pausing for thought. I looked at Mae, eyes wide. Where had that come from?

"Go on," she prompted with a half-smile.

I gulped air. "My mom and David were killed by a drunk driver. I don't think I said that before. This guy was totally hammered in the middle of the day and decided to drive home. He ran a red light and plowed into my mom's car and killed them both on impact. They didn't do anything wrong and they were killed.

Because of his one dumb choice, my family was gone, just like that," I snapped my fingers.

"And I bet you think that if you don't let people close, it won't hurt so much if that sort of thing happens again," Mae summarized.

"I guess so," I whispered. I hadn't had the words for it before this.

Mae reached over and took my hand, giving it a warm squeeze. "Is it ever hard for you to trust God because of that?"

"Sometimes," I admitted.

She sighed. "Life is so much more complicated than it should be."

"No kidding. I think that, by avoiding letting people get close, I'm trying to simplify my life." I sat up a little straighter as that revelation sank in. "It's why I don't want to have a lot of possessions, either. I can just float through on the edges of life without ever really diving in."

"Like those water bugs that skate on the surface."

"Right."

"My parents are missionaries in Colombia, I think I told you that." Mae waited for my nod. "I grew up over there and saw a lot of really hard things happening. There was a woman who lost five babies to parasites in the water. It was awful. But she developed this amazing trust in God. She would testify in church that if God saw fit to take her babies, it must be for a good purpose."

"Wow."

"I know." My red-headed friend looked over the front yard, but I felt sure that she was picturing far-off places. "I know that your family situation was awful, too. I'm so sorry you had to live your life feeling so alone. However, I also truly believe that God can take all those hard situations and turn them into something beautiful. It happens all throughout the Bible. I heard a preacher once say, 'It's okay to not be okay, but it's not okay to stay that way.' You get to choose, Emily, whether that hardship becomes something that keeps you away from other people, or it makes you a stronger woman who's better able to love others."

We sat in silence then. I was lost in thought and couldn't have carried on a conversation if my life depended on it. Running from relationships was lonely, and it really only seemed to hurt me. Maybe that was why this was so hard: now it hurt Nate, too. I'd thought I was fine as I skated along the surface of life, but now that Nate was in the picture, it would affect him. The closer we got, the more complicated that became.

But what if I let myself fall in love with him, and he was taken from me? It would be awful. Yet, I also knew from experience that the world would go on. It would feel like my heart was ripped out, but as time went by, the pain would dull, and I would move on.

A new thought bloomed, and my heart picked up its pace. I would rather love Nate, and have him love me in return and lose him, than never have him in the first place.

When Rosa called that supper was ready, I stood up, stooped over, and gave Mae a hug. "Thank you," I whispered.

"Any time," she beamed back, emerald eyes twinkling.

16

I WAS a tad disappointed when I didn't see Nate at work the next few days. I texted to check on him, and he responded that he was wrapped up in work and couldn't get away. As much as I wanted to see him, I had to admit that I was thrilled that he was taking his job so seriously.

Because he'd been so busy, we only saw each other once, though we talked on the phone every evening. It made me look forward to my time at Just Horsing Around even more than usual. Nate's court-ordered time had finished the previous week, but he had decided to stay on as a long-term volunteer. He was no longer able to come during the week, but he was committed to volunteering on Saturday afternoons. I missed seeing him on Tuesdays and was that much happier to see him on Saturdays.

That particular day, though, there wasn't time for

more than a quick smile and a hug before Dave called us all together.

"We've got a particularly challenging group today," he began. "This crew is coming to us from Jackson. We've had them before."

"Is it the class of autistic kids? The one with the crazy parents?" Jake clarified.

At Dave's affirmation, the others moaned.

"What?" I inquired, completely at sea.

"The kids are fine. Squirrelly, but fine," Sarah explained. "But they all come with their parents, and they are awful."

"One mother told me off for holding her child's hand since I had probably contracted germs from the horses." Chloe's raised eyebrows and rolling eyes told me exactly what she thought of that. "I mean, I was holding her kid's hand so I could help her get into the saddle and *ride a horse*."

"Okay, okay," Dave jumped in. He waved his hands in a 'let's all calm down' gesture. "Remember that our focus is on the children. No matter how their parents act, we want the children to enjoy themselves and be safe."

I exchanged a dark look with Chloe just as the van arrived from Jackson. The doors opened, and children exploded out on both sides. This was an excited group, that was for sure. Their parents began to arrive in their private cars not long after. Most sported designer label clothes, leather handbags, and enormous cups of coffee.

It took all of our best efforts to get the kids into their seats. They exclaimed over everything, which made it especially fun when Jake brought in Strawberry for the safety talk. The kids squealed and clapped. Strawberry was a very patient horse, and she gave the noisy bunch little notice.

The parents of the group were either absorbed in their phones or looking at the horse as though she was a bomb just waiting to go off. When people decided to bring their kids to Just Horsing Around, not all the parents were on board. Usually, though, by the time they left, they'd changed their tunes. I wasn't sure if that would prove to be true with this group.

Soon, we were heading to the barn to get helmets and start the ride. We didn't use all the horses every time. Only a few of them were able to handle the needs of these special kids. Other horses were used for more experienced riders who came to the ranch. There was a paddock for young riders where the kids could ride around and around in a big oval. The horses seemed content to patiently clop with the shrieks of excited kids on their backs. The rest of the horses used another, larger paddock closer to the stables. Some of the kids liked to stand at the fence, watching as those animals nibbled the grass and ran around.

The first group of riders needed a lot of help to get going. Several of the kids were scared of the horses and didn't want to go first. Sarah took over with them, and they went to get familiar with Honey, one of our gentle retired mares. Jake, Chloe, Nate, and I were busy helping the braver kids climb into their saddles. Few of the parents were interested in helping their children, and I began to understand why the staff had been groaning.

I was helping a little girl named Makayla, who was nonverbal. She seemed to understand what I was saying to her despite her reticence to speak, since she kept her heels down in the stirrups just fine after I showed her what to do. However, whenever something startled her, she dropped the reins.

"Makayla, how about I hold the reins and lead Midnight while you ride? Hold on to the saddle horn, here." I repositioned her hands.

We joined the other horses and plodded around the paddock. Makayla was soon grinning and would let go of the saddle horn to clap her hands when she was especially pleased with herself. I couldn't stop smiling whenever she did that, delighted in her enjoyment.

One of the boys kept calling to his mother, who was standing by the fence, "Look at me, Mom! Look at me!" She took a number of photos of him with her phone and waved back whenever he called to her.

A small clutch of mothers stood together, talking with elaborate hand gestures, not caring at all what their children were doing. I pursed my lips and worked hard at not being judgmental. I reminded myself that having kids was a lot of work, and these ladies were due a bit of rest. I told myself that their children were in our capable hands. And still I gave them the evil eye each time we passed.

Then it was time to switch. We helped the kids climb down and tried to discern which of our more timid guests would be willing to ride.

"Now, Ethan, this is why we came," one of the moms wheedled. "You need to give it a try."

I gave her a bracing smile when she looked my way. It could be a hard call to make. Some kids ended up loving it when they got up on the horse's back. Some cried until they were allowed to get down. We tried to let the children and their parents decide if the child should ride. I was relieved to notice that I wasn't feeling all judgy about this mother. At least I wasn't being unfair to all the parents.

A sudden movement to my left drew my attention. I looked over and saw that Makayla was running toward the paddock where the other horses were roaming free. I waited, watching to see what would happen. If she just wanted to stand at the fence and watch them, no harm would come to her. However, if she tried to climb through the fence, she could be in real danger.

The moment she put her hand on the fencepost and ducked to climb through, I took off running toward her.

"Stop, Makayla!" I yelled.

Either she hadn't heard me, or she was ignoring me.

She lifted her leg and, after a couple of attempts, slid it between the rails. Then she shifted her weight and was on the other side.

I arrived at the fence as she took off running through the paddock. I threw myself over the fence and tore after her. She was headed straight toward a huge, chestnut stallion named Horatio.

"Please, oh please," I prayed as I ran. If the horse ignored her, I could get her back to safety, but if she frightened him, he might bite her or kick her.

I was gaining on the girl. I would be able to grab her in just another few steps. But like a slow-motion movie, I watched as the enormous horse registered us running at him. He rolled his eyes and bunched his muscles, ready to kick out when we went past.

"Stop, Makayla!" I screamed.

Startled by my scream, she slowed and looked back at me. It was all I needed. I grabbed her, pulling her to the side just as Horatio kicked back. If his hooves had made contact, Makayla would have been thrown, breaking a number of bones. As it was, I was able to hold her and roll her as we fell so that I landed on my side and rolled onto my back, taking her weight onto me.

Unfortunately, I threw out my free hand to stop the fall and knew instantly that I'd broken a bone when it collided with the ground. Sharp pain exploded up from my wrist even as the air was knocked out of me.

Jake and Nate arrived only a few moments later.

Jake scooped Makayla up and carried her back to safety. Nate knelt over me, where I was biting my lip to try and keep from crying out over my wrist, which felt like it was being stabbed with red-hot knives.

"Are you okay, Emily?" he panted.

"My wrist," was all I could squeak out, breathless from the pain and the fall.

Nate helped me to my feet and put an arm around my shoulders as we headed back to the fence. Hands patted my shoulders and people kept saying encouraging things, but my wrist was too painful for any of their words to register.

After a quick word with Dave, Nate ushered me to his Jeep, and I climbed in. He went to my car for my bag, and then was back almost before it registered in my pain-clouded brain that he was gone.

"We're going to Melbourne to the hospital," he explained. "Hold on, Em."

The car ride was a blur. In some ways it was much longer than a half-hour, and in other ways it was much shorter. Landmarks leapt past, though I couldn't understand how we weren't at the hospital yet.

Once there, things moved more quickly. Thankfully, there wasn't much of a wait, and I was taken back for x-rays. The young doctor quickly realized I was in too much pain to hear her words and, with a friendly flash of white teeth, turned her explanations to Nate. I was given some painkillers, and a cast was wrapped around my fingers and lower arm.

The pills made me groggy, and I dozed as we drove back to Bumblebee House. Jill was on hand. She took me from Nate and helped me upstairs and into bed.

When I awoke, my wrist was throbbing and it was growing dark outside. I turned on a light and blinked as I remembered what had happened. My first thought was: thank goodness Makayla was okay. I don't know what I would have done if she'd been hurt. It was infinitely better that I'd broken a bone than if that little girl had.

Clumsy with my new cast, I changed into a pair of comfy shorts and a 'Missouri - the Show Me State' t-shirt. Putting my hair into a ponytail proved too hard for my tired brain, so I took my hair elastic downstairs in search of someone to help.

I was surprised to see Nate sitting on the couch, watching TV with Rosemarie.

"Hey!" He lit up when he saw me. "How are you feeling?"

"My wrist hurts," I mumbled.

Nate checked his phone. "Yeah, it's time for you to take another painkiller. Dr. Watkins said you'd want to make sure you took them for the first few days, at least."

"I can't put my hair up," I whined and held the elastic out to Rosemarie.

"I can help," she said and jumped up. "Everyone at the ranch was talking about how brave you were."

I shrugged. "Anyone would have done what I did."

"Well, thank goodness you saw that little girl when you did." Rosemarie expertly put my hair up into a tidy bun on the top of my head, and then gave me a little push toward the couch where Nate had been sitting.

He was back in an instant with a glass of water and a pill, which I threw back gratefully. Then, I was all too happy to curl up next to him, my head on his shoulder.

"Are you hungry?" he asked and kissed the top of my head.

I shook my head. "Just tired."

We watched whatever was on TV in silence for the next few minutes. I drifted off, the noise from the TV coming and going through my conscious brain like weak radio signals.

When I awoke, Rosemarie and Nate were having a very serious discussion. I kept my eyes closed and just listened.

"Yeah, it's not like with Shannon," Nate was saying.

"Really? The two of you were so serious back in high school." Rosemarie's voice was quiet but intense.

"I thought we were, too." Nate sighed. "But what you think is love when you're that young isn't like the real thing."

"And you know that because…?"

I felt Nate nod. "I know what it is to be in love now. I didn't before Emily."

In my hazy, fresh-from-sleep, painkiller-filled mental place, my heart fluttered. Nate was telling Rosemarie that he loved me. With my cheek on his shoulder and his arm around me, I knew there was nowhere else I wanted to be.

"Wow, Nate. I'm really happy for you," Rosemarie said.

He changed the subject. "Whatever happened with that friend of Matt's? Ty, wasn't it? I thought you were crazy about him."

"Nothing ever happened. I mean, he was my brother's best friend." Despite her protestations, Rosemarie seemed flustered.

Silence stretched. Then my housemate gently said, "If you're in love with Emily, what do you see happening in the future? I was under the impression that she's planning to move on sometime next year."

Nate's hand tightened slightly on my arm. In a voice that was so full of emotion that it squeezed my heart, he answered softly, "I wish I knew. And, you know, it's killing me."

17

IT TOOK two days before I felt like myself again and another full day before I began functioning mostly as usual, with my hand in a cast. Word had spread as to what had happened, and everyone who came into the Beanery on my first day back had something to say about it.

"You're such a brave girl," Mrs. Jennings cooed and patted my good arm as she took her cup of tea from me. "Thank goodness you were there."

I smiled my thanks wearily. Sophie had started the shift with me, since Matt couldn't be there first thing in the morning. It had taken some doing, but I was figuring out how to compensate for my reduced motion. At first, Sophie had insisted on doing everything. That had lasted all of one order before I told her in no uncertain terms that I would be pulling my weight if it killed me.

I had then proceeded to knock over the change jar, sending it rolling off the counter, where it smashed spectacularly on the original wood floors. Sophie had helped me pick the coins from the rubble and then swept up, since handling a broom was beyond me. Still, by noon I was doing better, and she had left me at the end of her shift with little more than a single check over her shoulder that I was surviving without her.

Things had quieted down, and I fixed myself a cup of cold-brew coffee over ice to combat my tiredness and the heat of the late-July day outside, which kept creeping in whenever the door swung open with its usual cheerful jangle.

I had my back to the door, pouring cream and sugar in my coffee, when the familiar bells announced a new customer. I turned back and saw a very pretty woman about my age wearing a fabulous professional pencil skirt, swiss dotted blouse, and trendy blazer. Her six-inch heels clicked neatly as she came closer. I admired her perfect makeup and gorgeous, rich chestnut hair whose curls bounced with each step.

"Hi," I greeted her with a smile. I was wearing my new jeans, a slightly discolored Beanery v-neck, and no makeup. Yet, I felt no competitive rush. This woman was beautiful. Good for her. "What can I get you?"

"I'd like a soy latte with skim milk, please," she ordered breezily.

As I began to fix her drink, I felt her eyes on me. Usually, put-together young professional women were quick to put their attention back on their phones just as soon as they could. I wondered what it was that was drawing her gaze.

I handed her the steaming cup and she paused, lips pursed.

"I don't mean to pry, but you are the Emily who's dating Nate Weisert, aren't you?"

I blinked in surprise. "Yes," I said slowly.

She stuck out a beautifully manicured hand. "I'm Shannon Eargle. Nate and I dated back in high school."

I rubbed my sticky hand on my apron before putting it into hers. "Nice to meet you."

Shannon bit her lip and, for the first time, seemed unsure of herself. "I came in here because I wanted to tell you something about Nate."

A rock fell into my stomach. "Okay," I replied, crossing my arms.

She put up her hand, eyes wide, "Oh, I'm not trying to warn you away from him or anything. He and I dated so long ago. I'm not after him, I swear."

"You're making me nervous. What are you here for?" I tried to smile.

She gave a little laugh before taking a deep breath. "I ran into him the other day, and I was really impressed. He seems like a whole new person. A better person, really. When he mentioned you, he was glowing. I'm so happy for him.

"When we dated back in high school, he was trying so hard to be the person everyone wanted him to be that he was miserable. I don't think he even realized how unhappy he really was." She looked down and shook her head. "I live in Melbourne now. I'm engaged." She held out her left hand, where a large diamond glinted.

"Congrats," I said genuinely.

"Thanks. Anyway, when I was driving by, I figured I'd stop in and tell you how glad I am that you're dating him. After he and I split up, he ran around with a few girls, I think, in college. He never seemed able to find a direction for his life. Then there was that whole drunk driving thing, and I was afraid that he was going to throw his life away."

My heart stopped. I swear it did. Numbly, I heard myself ask, "What drunk driving thing?"

Shannon's eyes widened. "Didn't you know? Oh, I'm so sorry. I assumed he'd told you. I don't know if I'm the one who should say anything."

I reached out my good hand and grabbed her wrist. "Please tell me what you know."

"Okay," she said slowly. "Nate went to Melbourne to a car dealership and test-drove a super expensive, top-of-the-line truck. He was allowed to take it out on his own, since his dad knew the owner. He picked up a friend and they started drinking. I guess they were off-roading and having a good time. But when they came back on Highway 30e, he lost control and totaled the truck."

I froze, my brain refusing to process this new

information.

Shannon looked at me and misread the signs. "Oh, it's okay, Emily, really. He didn't go to jail for it or anything. His dad worked it out so he could just do community service hours, and he paid for the truck to smooth things over." She looked at me and grew concerned. "Should I have told you all that?"

I think I nodded. "Thanks," I mumbled.

"Sure. Anyway, I'm glad he has you now. I guess I should get going." And she clicked her way back to her car.

I almost ran to the back of the store, where I stood in the storeroom, shaking. Nate had totaled a car driving drunk. He'd been a drunk driver. All I could think of was the moment when my dad had come into my room, sat on the bed next to me, and told me that a drunk driver had killed my mom and my brother. And Nate was one.

I felt like I'd been punched in the gut. I couldn't breathe, I couldn't cry, I couldn't think what to say or do.

The bells jingled up front, and I tried to calm myself enough to get back to work. As I stepped out from the storeroom, I heard Matt calling my name as he came back toward his office.

"I have to go," I stammered.

My boss looked instantly worried. "Is it your arm?"

"Yes," I lied immediately.

"Okay, no problem. I'm here now."

I all but sprinted to the door. I had to get away before Nate came in. It would be just my luck that he'd decide to suddenly take a coffee break. There was no way I could face him in this state.

I'd driven to work and so, I jumped in my van and drove home, unsure of how I'd gotten there once I pulled to a stop in the driveway.

"Oh, good, you're home," Rosa said when I came in the door. "Dave from Just Horsing Around called earlier. He asked for you to call him back."

Hollowly, I went to the kitchen and dialed Dave's number, thinking all the while that it was pointless. I wouldn't be able to hear what he had to say.

"Thanks for calling me back, Emily," he said. If I hadn't been so distracted, I would have noticed that his voice was unusually solemn. "Listen, I've got some bad news."

"Bad news?" I echoed.

"I'm sorry, but I'm going to have to ask you not to come back to Just Horsing Around for a little while."

I stood there, trying to make sense of his words. "What?"

Dave was apologetic. "Makayla's mother is threatening to sue the ranch and our program and, well, and you. She's trying to say that there was some gross neglect on our part that allowed her daughter to almost get hurt.

"Now, don't get me wrong, Emily, I'm glad you did

what you did. However, until we get this straightened out, we need you to take some time off."

I hung up woodenly without saying goodbye. Then I turned and marched up the stairs and began packing. It was easier to stop my brain from thinking and simply fill boxes and suitcases. I was surprised at how clearly and unemotionally I could look around the room for anything I'd forgotten. It took more trips up and down the stairs than when I'd moved in, since I was doing it with one hand, and alone.

I stood in the kitchen with the ever-present pad of cheery bumblebee-bordered stationery, trying to think what to write. Finally I scribbled, 'I have to go. Thanks for everything. - Emily.'

The house was silent as I left. I climbed into my van, heart full, and turned the key. I had no plan. No idea where I was going next. I just knew I had to get away.

As I headed off down the highway, I turned the radio on loudly enough that it filled my ears and silenced any protests my good sense could make. But I couldn't stop my brain from flipping through everything that was wrong.

I was being blamed for what had happened with Makayla.

Nate had totaled a car driving drunk.

I was leaving the first home I'd had since I was eight.

I had nowhere to go.

I hadn't gone more than ten miles before my

emotions defrosted. I pulled over into an abandoned gas station and turned my car off. Instantly, I began sobbing.

As I cried, I poured my heart out in prayer. "Why, God?" I moaned. "Why is everything so awful? Why did all this have to happen? Why would that woman blame me when I saved her daughter from harm? Why did Nate have to be a drunk driver, of all things? What am I supposed to do now?"

Around and around I went, revisiting each wound until my tears subsided and I was left searching for tissues for my runny nose, the occasional shudder running through my body.

In the quiet, Rosa's words came back to me. I remembered how she'd affirmed that relationships were messy. People, by default, would always hurt each other. What had she said? Oh, yes. We needed grace and forgiveness. I thought of Mae's story of the woman in Colombia who had lost her babies and still praised God.

I leaned my head back against the head rest, exhausted. "What am I supposed to do now, God?" I whispered. Then, for the first time in a long time, I sat silently. I didn't try to argue why I should be allowed to leave. I didn't explain that I loved Nate but couldn't be with him. I didn't even try to figure out a plan for what was coming next. I just sat in the oddly holy silence in my old maroon minivan.

I didn't have an epiphany. No visions came to me. I

didn't hear a still, small whisper. But I knew what to do.

It was time to go home.

Bumblebee House was still silent when I got there. My note was still on the kitchen counter, untouched and unread. Gratefully, I tore it off the pad and crumpled it in my hand. I tipped it into the garbage can with a sigh of relief.

Then I did penance by toting all my possessions back upstairs, one-handed, and putting them all away. I was exhausted, but I needed to reach out to Nate before I let myself take a nap. I pulled out my phone and texted, asking that he meet me that night. I said it was really important.

I stripped off my sweaty shorts and tank top and slid between the cool sheets. My phone pinged, and I read that Nate would pick me up at seven. Then I rolled over and slept a deep, restful sleep.

That night at supper, I ate quietly, looking over each

of the Bumblebee girls—the girls I had almost left behind forever just a few short hours before. Maybe it was my newfound appreciation, but they seemed even lovelier than usual. Angels in tank tops and bare feet.

Jill was complaining that her laundry pile was getting huge again. Rosemarie rolled her eyes with a gentle grin. Mae teased Jill about finding some weird outfit to wear when she saw Marco the following weekend. Rosa laughed merrily at their antics.

When they asked me why I was so quiet, I shrugged and said I was tired. Rosemarie offered to take over cleaning up for me, since I couldn't wash the dishes. I hugged her and felt the enormous peace and gratitude that came with finally being home. I knew that it was a temporary place. Who knew how long we would all live at Bumblebee House? But for now, tonight, this was my home, and these were my people, and I couldn't have been happier to be there.

I was waiting on the porch when Nate arrived. I strolled to the Jeep and climbed in.

"Where should we go?" he asked, though I could tell he was dying to ask what it was that I needed to talk to him about.

"Can we go back to that rock? You know the one, right?"

He smiled. "I sure do. Hang on."

The wind whipped my hair in its ponytail, and I rested my right hand on the door as Nate drove, letting the wind push against my fingers. I had so many things to say to Nate. Some of them would hurt him, but I had faith that we would be okay. Even if we weren't, even if he was angry and we stopped dating, I would be fine. I had my work at the Beanery, my sisters at Bumblebee House. I belonged here in Birch Springs even without Nate, though I sure hoped I would still have him after tonight.

We climbed to the rock, which was still warm from the sun's rays. This time, when Nate sat down and leaned back, I didn't curl up with him. I sat on the other side, one leg dangling down over the edge of the rock.

"You're killing me, Em," Nate said, almost teasing. "What's up?"

I folded my hands primly in my lap, carefully cradling my cast. "I need to tell you some things, and I need you to just listen. You're going to want to talk, but you can't right now. Okay?"

"That's not helping," he groaned. Then he pulled himself together and said, "Okay, okay. I'll be quiet, just tell me what's going on."

"Your ex-girlfriend, Shannon, came into the coffee shop today." I held out a hand when he opened his mouth. "Stop. I get to talk right now. Shannon only had good things to say. She came in because she wanted to tell me how happy you seemed when she last spoke to you.

"But then she told me about why you had community service hours." I licked my lips and looked away. "I didn't know what to say. I had no idea that you had been driving drunk. Nate, when I heard that, I… I sort of fell apart."

I hugged my arms around myself and went on. "You know what happened to my family. I've spent my entire life hating the fact that anyone would be so selfish as to get wasted, get in a car, and put other people's lives in danger.

"I lost more than my mother and my brother that day. I lost my family. I lost my home. The past eighteen years, I've just been floating through life without anything tying me down because some guy had too much to drink and thought he could drive himself home." Tears were falling, and I couldn't bring myself to look at Nate. "When I heard that you had made that same choice, I thought it was over. I actually went home and packed my stuff and left town."

I could see out of the corner of my eye that Nate's mouth had dropped open, and he'd sat up at those words. But he kept quiet, and I went on.

"I guess you could say that God got ahold of me at an abandoned Shell station on Highway 30. I started thinking about things that Rosa and Mae have said to me, and something changed. The death of my mom and brother were horrible, but I know God's bigger. He can use them in a good way, somehow. So, maybe God can use what you did for good, too. Who am I to hold something against you that God has already forgiven?"

I finally looked up at Nate, who took that question as the end of my soliloquy. He scrambled over the rock until he was next to me and took my unbroken hand carefully in his.

"He did use it for good," Nate said fervently. "If I hadn't been an idiot and done that ridiculous thing, I wouldn't have been at the ranch, and you wouldn't have told me off that day, and I wouldn't have finally reevaluated my life. It was your words, Em, that changed things for me. I joined that men's Bible study. I started going in to work. And you stopped looking at me like I was the most disgusting specimen of manhood that ever existed."

"Did I really look at you like that?" I gaped at him.

He shrugged. "I deserved it. Anyway, that's not the point. Emily, before you came here, I hated myself and I didn't even know it. Everything I touched seemed to wither and die. I was this hollow shell, trying not to let anything get close enough to see how miserable I was. But you saw, and you cut right through to the root of it all."

He shifted until he was sitting with one leg behind me and the other bent, our knees touching, our faces only inches apart. "I've been wanting to say this for a long time, but I was afraid it would make you mad." His eyes checked mine quickly, and then he nodded and went on. "Please don't leave. Don't leave me. Ever.

I know it's too soon for me to ask you to marry me, but I plan on it. If you want to leave and go have adventures discovering new places, I want to go with you. I am in love with you, Emily McBride, and not because you're beautiful, even though you are. It's because of how honest you are and how much you care for people and how you fight for what's right. You're smart and funny, and you don't care about the stupid rules other people make up. I've never loved anyone the way I love you."

I looked into his fervent, lovely sea-green eyes and gave him a wobbly smile. "I love you, too."

"You do?" His face broke into a huge, hopeful grin, and I felt like I'd given him the world.

My smile widened. "With my whole heart. I love how kind you are. I love that you genuinely love people. You faced up to your faults and have turned your life around. That inspires me. Plus, you're a total babe."

Nate's hands came up, and he held my face tenderly, and then leaned forward and placed a kiss on my lips. He pulled back, but one kiss wasn't enough, and he came back for a second, which quickly became a third.

I'd forgotten everything except his lips on mine and his hands on my face and my pounding heart when he set me back determinedly.

"Oh, that's going to be a problem," he groaned.

"What is?" I asked, suddenly afraid that I was a terrible kisser and had never known it.

"We're going to have to be very careful, or else I'm not going to be able to keep control."

I smiled and, for the first time in my life, the thought of settling down with someone didn't terrify me. Not only that, I could actually picture it happening. How did this guy break through the barriers around my heart so quickly?

He might have thought I had come along and changed his life, but he did the same to mine. Already my life was better because of Nate. And this was just the beginning.

I DRESSED for the gala with the help of Mae.

"The limo's here," Jill called up the stairs.

"How do I look?" I asked Mae.

Her eyes crinkled and she said, "My sister, you are a rare work of art."

I smiled at her, surprised at that response. "I like that. Thank you, Mae. But, to be honest, you are a rare work of art, too."

"Oh, I know." She laughed her tinkling laugh.

I gave her a careful hug and went in search of my sandals. The other Bumblebee girls were waiting and had hugs and compliments, too.

I stopped in front of Rosa, who looked me over. I wanted her approval, knowing how good she was with clothes and shoes.

Her smile spoke of understanding more than just what was going on in that moment. Her dark eyes sparkled as she said, "I'm so glad you decided to stick around, Emily."

"You were right. I already feel like a millionaire."

She pulled me into a hug. "And you've only just begun."

I whirled out the door, tugging my shoes on as I went, clutch in hand. Nate had climbed out of the limo and stood leaning against it. He looked amazing in his tuxedo. That boy was just too handsome for words.

His eyes lit up with delight when he saw me. He whistled playfully. "My, my, Miss McBride, you are a vision!"

I gave him a quick kiss, and then hopped into the limo where his parents and sister were waiting. They looked over my dress, and their smiles became wooden.

"You look lovely," I complimented the ladies, meaning every word. "What gorgeous gowns."

"Thank you," Lucy said stiffly before turning the conversation to other things.

Nate and I exchanged an amused look. I had found my dress at a Bibles for Missions thrift shop. It was simple, made of a shiny, black fabric. It fell just past my knees and had an empire waist. It was absolutely perfect for me, and absolutely not the sort of thing one wore to a gala. But Rosa had cut some flowers for my hair, and Mae had curled it before pinning it into a halo. I felt beautiful and true to myself.

As the limo turned onto the highway, Nate and I snuggled back into our seats, lost in our own hazy happiness.

"You look good," he said, a note of teasing in his voice. "Maybe a little too good. I don't want some other fellow to come along and take you away."

"You'd better be extra nice to me, then," I teased back. "I'd probably go willingly with whatever guy came along."

"I guess I should do something so everyone knows you're taken," he whispered in my ear.

"Like what? A brand across my forehead? A leash?" I said playfully.

"How about this?" He reached into his coat pocket and pulled out a velvet box.

I sat up straighter and looked at him, completely taken by surprise.

"Open it," he prompted with a chuckle.

I took the box and opened the lid. Inside was a silver ring with three round emeralds. It was beautiful. "Oh, Nate," I breathed.

"I know you're not ready to get married, but I wanted to give you something that makes you think of me, and hopefully our future together."

He slipped the ring from the box and held it out to me. I gave him my left hand and nodded as he slipped it over my finger. Not wanting to alert his family to our private moment, I beamed at him, and then leaned in for another kiss.

"I won't hassle you about marriage," he said as he looked into my eyes. "But promise me you'll let me know when you're ready to talk about it."

"It's a deal," I answered. Then I settled back against him, gazing at my beautiful ring and knowing that, right here, with Nate, I was home.

THANK YOU

Thanks for reading my book. I hope you enjoyed reading the story as much as I enjoyed writing it. If you did, or even if you didn't, it would be awesome if you left a review for me on Amazon and/or Goodreads. It really helps me know how I'm doing.

The next book in the Triple Star Ranch Romance series is called *Learning to Love* and you will definitely want to find out who learns to love next.

Order ***Learning to Love*** on Amazon

And if you're interested in historical western stories, you should check out the Rushing Into Love series which takes place during the California Gold Rush. The first story in that series is called *More Precious Than Gold*.

Get *More Precious Than Gold* on Amazon.

Before I go, I would like to offer you SIX FREE BOOKS. Check out the details on the next page.

Make sure you sign up for our Sweet Romance Newsletter so you can keep up with our latest releases. We have everything from historical western romance to contemporary romance. All of it sweet and clean. When you sign up, we will send you six of our best inspirational stories - FOR FREE!

fairfieldpublishing.com/western-romance-newsletter/